THE READER ON THE 6.27

JEAN-PAUL DIDIERLAURENT

Translated by Ros Schwartz

THE READER ON THE 6.27

MANTLE

First published 2015 by Mantle
an imprint of Pan Macmillan, a division of Macmillan Publishers Limited
Pan Macmillan, 20 New Wharf Road, London N1 9RR
Basingstoke and Oxford
Associated companies throughout the world
www.panmacmillan.com

ISBN 978-1-4472-7646-3

Originally published in French 2014 as *Le Liseur du 6h27* by Au diable vauvert, 2014

The right of Jean-Paul Didierlaurent to be identified as the
author of this work has been asserted by him in accordance
with the Copyright, Designs and Patents Act 1988.

This is a work of fiction. Names, characters, places, organizations and
incidents are either products of the author's imagination or used fictitiously.
Any resemblance to actual events, places, organizations or persons,
living or dead, is entirely coincidental.

9 8 7 6 5 4 3 2 1

A CIP catalogue record for this book is available from the British Library.

Printed and bound by CPI Group (UK) Ltd, Croydon, CR0 4YY

Visit **www.panmacmillan.com** to read more about all our books
and to buy them. You will also find features, author interviews and
news of any author events, and you can sign up for e-newsletters
so that you're always first to hear about our new releases.

Thank you to Sabine,

without whom this book would not exist,

to my father,

who, through his invisible presence,

continues to inspire me with his eternal

love,

and to Colette,

for her constant support.

THE READER ON THE 6.27

1

Some people are born deaf, mute or blind. Others come into the world afflicted by a nasty squint, a harelip or an unsightly strawberry mark in the middle of their face. And then there are those who emerge with a club foot, or a limb that's already dead before it's even lived. As for Guylain Vignolles, he began his life encumbered only by his name, which lent itself to an unfortunate spoonerism: Vilain Guignol – ugly puppet – a bad pun that rang in his ears from the moment he first drew breath, and quickly stuck.

His parents had shunned all the saints' names

listed in the 1976 post office calendar and plucked Guylain out of thin air, not stopping for one moment to think about the disastrous consequences of their choice. Strangely enough, even though he often felt extremely curious about it, Guylain had never dared to ask the reason. Afraid of causing embarrassment perhaps. Afraid too that the banality of the reply would most likely leave him disappointed. He sometimes tried to imagine what his life might have been like had he been called Lucas, Xavier or Hugo. He would even have been content with Ghislain. Ghislain Vignolles, a proper name that would have allowed him to make something of himself, his body and mind well shielded by four inoffensive syllables. Instead, he'd had to go through his childhood dogged by the humiliating spoonerism Vilain Guignol.

During his thirty-six years, he had perfected the art of melting into the background and becoming invisible so as to avoid sparking off the laughter and mockery that never failed to erupt as soon as his presence was noticed. His aim was to be neither good-looking nor ugly, neither fat nor thin. Just a vague shape hovering on the edge of people's field of vision. To blend into his surroundings until he negated himself, remaining a remote place never visited. During all those years, Guylain Vignolles had spent his time quite simply not existing, apart from on this dismal station platform where he stood every weekday morning.

Each day at the same time he waited for his train, both feet on the white line that must not be crossed at the peril of falling onto the track. That insignificant line on the concrete had a strangely soothing effect on him. Here the stench of death that constantly fogged his brain evaporated as if by magic. During the few minutes before the arrival of the train, he stamped his feet as if trying to sink into the concrete, fully aware that this was merely an illusory reprieve, that the only way to escape the barbarism that lay beyond the horizon was to move away from that line on which he stood awkwardly shifting from one foot to the other, and to go home. He could quite simply give up, go back to bed and curl up in the still-warm hollow made by his body during the night. Escape into sleep. But in the end, Guylain always reconciled himself to toeing the white line, listening to the little crowd of regular commuters gathering behind him, their eyes on the back of his neck causing a tingling that reminded him he was still alive. Over the years, the other passengers had come to show him the indulgent respect reserved for harmless nutters. Guylain was a breath of fresh air who, for the duration of the twenty-minute journey, allowed them briefly to forget the tedium of their lives.

2

The train pulled into the platform with a screech of brakes. Guylain tore himself from the white line and stepped into the compartment. The narrow folding seat to the right of the door awaited him. He preferred the hard orange plastic flap to the softness of the plush seats. The jump seat had become part of the ritual. There was something symbolic about the act of lowering his seat that he found reassuring. As the compartment began to sway, he took the cardboard folder out of the leather briefcase that never left his side. He opened it cautiously and exhumed a piece of paper from between two sheets of candy-pink blotting paper. The flimsy, half-torn page with a tattered top left-hand corner dangled from his fingers. It was a page from a standard six-by-nine-inch format book. Guylain examined it for a moment then placed it carefully back on the blotting paper. The carriage gradually fell silent. Sometimes, there was a reproving 'Shh' to silence the few conversations that had not petered out. Then, as he did every morning, Guylain cleared his throat and began reading aloud:

'*The child stood there, dumbstruck. He had eyes only for the twitching animal hanging from the barn door. The man's hand moved closer to its quivering throat. The slender blade plunged silently into the white down and a warm jet spurted from the wound, splattering his wrist with bright red droplets. With his sleeves rolled up to the elbows, the father slashed the fur with a few deft movements. Then, his strong hands slowly tugged at the fur, which peeled off like a sock, exposing the rabbit's streamlined, muscular body in all its nakedness, still steaming from its life cut short. Its head lolled, ugly and bony, its two protruding eyes staring into the void without even a hint of reproach.*'

As daylight barged against the misted-up windows, the words poured out of his mouth in a long string of syllables, occasionally punctuated by silences that engulfed the rattling of the train. For all those fellow commuters, he was the reader, the bizarre character who each weekday would read out, in a loud, clear voice, from the handful of pages he extracted from his briefcase. These were completely unrelated fragments of books. Part of a recipe might find itself teamed up with page forty-eight of the latest Goncourt winner, or a paragraph from a crime novel might follow a page from a history book. Guylain had no interest in the content. Only the act of reading mattered to him. He enunciated the words whatever they were with the same passionate dedication. And each time, the magic worked. As the words left his mouth they bore away a little of the nausea that suffocated him as he neared the plant:

'*Finally, the blade revealed the mystery. The father made a long incision in the animal's belly and scooped out the steaming entrails. The string of intestines slithered out, as if impatient to leave the ribcage where they had been confined. All that was left of the rabbit was a tiny, bloody body swaddled in a tea towel. A few days later, a new rabbit appeared. Another ball of white fur that hopped around in the stifling hutch, with the same blood-red eyes that stared at the child from beyond the realm of the dead.'*

Without even looking up, Guylain delicately extricated a new sheet:

'In a desperate bid to escape, the men had instinctively flung themselves face downwards, pressing deeper and deeper into the bosom of the protective earth. Some scraped away the soil with their bare hands, like mad dogs. Others curled into a ball and offered their fragile spines to the deadly shrapnel raining down on them. All were huddled up – a reflex as old as time. All except Josef, that is – he had remained on his feet amid the mayhem and, in an insane gesture, had thrown his arms around the trunk of a tall silver birch facing him. The tree oozed a thick resin through the gashes streaking its trunk, fat tears of sap that beaded on the surface of the bark then seeped slowly downwards. The tree was emptying itself, just like Josef, whose burning urine was streaming down his thighs. With each new explosion, the birch quivered against his cheek and trembled in his embrace.'

Guylain scrutinized the dozen or so pages ex-humed from his briefcase until the train drew into the station. As the echo of the last words he had uttered died away on the roof of his mouth, he looked up at his fellow commuters for the first time since boarding the train. He encountered disap-pointment, sadness even, on their faces, as he often did. It was as fleeting as the swish of a horse's tail. The compartment emptied quickly. He too rose. His seat snapped shut. The end. A middle-aged woman whispered a shy 'thank you'. Guylain smiled at her. How could he explain that he wasn't doing this for them? Resignedly, he quit the warmth of the train, leaving the day's pages behind him. He loved knowing that they were stuffed snugly between the base and the back of the folding seat, far from the murderous din from which they had been rescued. Outside, the rain was pelting down even harder. As always, walking towards the works, he heard old Giuseppe's grating voice in his head. *You're not cut out for this, kiddo. You don't know it yet, but you're not cut out for it!* The old boy knew what he was talking about. He had never found anything better than red plonk to give him the strength to go on. Guylain hadn't taken any notice, naively believing that in

3

The gate squeaked gratingly when he pushed it open to enter the works. The noise jolted the security guard, who looked up from his book. The 1936 reprint of Racine's *Britannicus* which he was holding was so well thumbed that it looked like a wounded bird. Guylain wondered whether Yvon Grimbert ever left his post. He appeared to be blithely oblivious to the discomfort of this flimsy three-by-two-metre shelter at the mercy of the elements, as long as the big plastic storage box containing his books was always by his side. He was fifty-nine, with classical theatre the only true love of his life, and it was not unusual, between two deliveries, to see him slip into the role of Don Diego or drape himself in the toga of an imaginary Pyrrhus, his powerful arms sweeping the air of his cramped hut, abandoning for the duration of an impassioned speech his thankless role that consisted of raising or lowering the red and white barrier at the entrance to the works, for which he earned a pittance. Always dapperly dressed, Yvon was particularly meticulous when it came to grooming the pencil moustache that adorned his upper lip, never missing an opportunity to quote the great Cyrano de Bergerac: 'All words are fair that lurk 'neath fair moustache!'

The day he had discovered the alexandrine, Yvon Grimbert had fallen head over heels in love. Faithfully serving the twelve-syllable line had become his sole mission on earth. Guylain liked Yvon for his wackiness. For that, and perhaps too because he was one of the few people not to have succumbed to the temptation of calling him Vilain Guignol.

'Morning, Monsieur Grimbert.'

'Morning, kiddo.'

Like Giuseppe, Yvon insisted on calling Guylain 'kiddo'.

'Fatso and Dumbo are already here,' he said. Yvon

always referred to them in that order and never the other way around. Fatso before Dumbo. When he wasn't versifying, the security guard spoke in terse sentences, not because he was sparing with words but because he preferred to save his voice for the only thing that was really worthwhile in his eyes: the alexandrine. As Guylain headed for the vast metal machine shed, Yvon recited two lines of his own composition at his receding form:

> 'The rain falls on my hut, sudden and mysterious,
> The drumming won't let up, loud as hail delirious.'

The Thing sat there, huge and menacing, right in the centre of the plant. In the fifteen years he had worked there, Guylain had never been able to call it by its real name, as if the simple act of naming it might be to acknowledge it, to demonstrate a sort of tacit acceptance, which he did not want at any cost. Refusing to name it was the last bastion he had managed to erect between it and himself, to avoid selling his soul to it for good. The Thing would have to be content with only his body. The name engraved on the colossus's steel side evoked the stench of imminent death: Zerstor 500, from the verb *zerstören*, which means 'to destroy' in Goethe's beautiful tongue. The Zerstor Fünfhundert was an eleven-tonne monstrosity produced in 1986 by the Krafft GmbH workshop, south of the Ruhr. The first time Guylain had seen it, the greyish-green colour of its metal shell had not really surprised him. What could be more natural than this warlike colour for a machine whose only purpose was to destroy? At first glance, it looked like a spray booth or a giant generator, a giant rotary printing press even, which was the ultimate irony. The Thing's sole apparent pretension seemed to be ugliness. But that was only the tip of the iceberg. In the middle of the grey concrete floor, the beast's gaping mouth formed a dark four-by-three-metre oblong leading to the unknown. There, sheltering in the dark, beneath a huge steel funnel, sat the fearsome contraption, a machine without which the plant would have been merely a useless warehouse.

On the technical side, the Zerstor 500's name was derived from the 500 hammers the size of men's fists arranged in alternating rows on the two horizontal cylinders covering the entire width of the tank. There were also 600 stainless-steel knives aligned along three axes and spinning at a speed of 800 revolutions per minute. On either side of this hell, twenty or so nozzles formed a guard of honour continually gushing 300-bar-high pressure jets of water at a temperature of 120°C. Then came the four powerful arms of the mixer in their stainless-steel casing. And finally, caged in its iron prison, the monstrous 1,000-horsepower diesel engine brought the entire machine to life. The Thing was born to crush, flatten, pound, squish, tear, chop, lacerate, shred, mix, knead and boil. But the best definition ever heard was the one old Giuseppe liked to yell when the plonk he guzzled all day long hadn't sufficiently dulled his visceral hatred for the Zerstor 500, stored up over the years: 'Genociiiiide!'

4

At this early hour, the plant had the chilling atmosphere of an empty ballroom. No trace remained of what had taken place there the previous day. Nor was there the slightest hint of the sound and fury that would erupt between those walls in the minutes to come. *Leave no clues.* That was one of Felix Kowalski's obsessions. Night after night, the boss had the scene of the crime cleaned so that it was always immaculate. A crime repeated over and over, every day of the year, apart from weekends and public holidays.

Guylain crossed the floor with reluctant steps.

Lucien Brunner was waiting for him. The young man in his always spotless overalls was leaning nonchalantly against the Thing's control panel. Arms folded across his chest, he greeted Guylain with his usual wry grin. Never a hello, never a gesture, just that arrogant smile bestowed with the superciliousness of a twenty-five-year-old who stood more than six feet tall. Brunner was forever sounding off for the benefit of anyone who cared to listen: civil servants were all lazy lefties; women were only good for waiting on their husbands, in other words cooking during the day and getting knocked up at night; immigrants (a word he chuntered rather than uttered) were taking the food out of French mouths. Not forgetting the stinking rich, benefits scroungers, corrupt politicians, Sunday drivers, junkies, poofters, junky poofters, the disabled and whores. Brunner had views on everything – very firm views which Guylain had long since given up attempting to challenge. For a while he had used rhetoric to try and explain to Brunner that things weren't quite so black and white; that in between there was a whole range of greys, from very pale to very dark. To no avail. Guylain had eventually come to terms with the fact that Brunner was an idiot beyond redemption. Beyond redemption and dangerous. Lucien Brunner was a dab hand at royally taking the piss out of you while licking your boots. His 'Monsieur Vignolles' tinged with condescension exuded a veiled contempt. Brunner was a serpent of the worst kind, a cobra ready to strike at the tiniest blunder. Guylain did his best to avoid him, keeping well away from his fangs. And worst of all, that arsehole loved his executioner's job.

'Hey, Monsieur Vignolles, will you let me turn the machine on today?'

Guylain gloated inwardly. No, M'sieur Vignolles was not going to allow him to turn the machine on today. Or tomorrow, or the next day! M'sieur Vignolles had no intention of affording him the immense pleasure that lay in the simple act of starting up that bitch of a machine! 'No, Brunner. You know very well that you can't until you've got the appropriate qualifications.' Guylain loved that expression, which he uttered in a compassionate tone, even though he was dreading the day when that moron would thrust the coveted licence under his nose. That day was not far off and then he would have to give in. Not a week went by without Brunner raising the matter with Kowalski, urging old Fatso to talk to management about his application. At every opportunity, that two-faced bastard would pester him, with his 'Monsieur Kowalski's and his 'Yes, Chief's, never missing a chance to poke his weasel face round the office door and butter him up. An oxpecker on the back of a buffalo. And Kowalski lapped it up. All that kowtowing flattered his vanity. Meanwhile, Guylain sheltered behind the regulations to lecture Brunner, always with the fleeting impression of goading a cobra with a stick. No qualification, no press button!

'For fuck's sake, Vignolles, start it up! What are you waiting for? The rain to stop?' Kowalski, who had spotted him from the top of his ivory tower, had burst out of his office to come and screech at him in his falsetto voice. His glazed eyrie was almost ten metres up in the air, suspended beneath the roof. From up there, Kowalski could see everything, like a little god keeping watch over his dominion. The slightest alert, the tiniest slip-up, and he'd come rushing out onto the bridge to yell his orders or to unleash a torrent of abuse. And if he felt that was not enough, as in this instance, he would come clattering down the thirty or so metal stairs which groaned under the weight of his mass of lard.

'Get a move on, Vignolles, damn it! There are already three lorries waiting outside.' Felix Kowalski didn't speak; he barked, yelled, bellowed, cursed and roared, but he had never been able to talk in a normal voice. He couldn't help it. He never began his day without directing a volley of abuse at the first person to come within earshot, as if the rancour that had built up inside him overnight had to escape from his mouth before it choked him. That first person was often Guylain. Brunner, who was stupid but not blind or deaf, had quickly twigged the boss's game and generally stayed out of sight behind the Zerstor's control cabinet. Fatso's tirades didn't bother Guylain one way or the other. They rarely lasted more than a minute. You just had to let them wash over you and wait until the tsunami was over. Pull your head in and wait until Kowalski had finished belching abuse in a cloud of sour sweat. Of course, Guylain sometimes felt like rebelling, or crying foul. Pointing out to that bile-spewing, pot-bellied brute that the big hand of the clock above the cloakroom door, the only one you could rely on according to Kowalski, was more than ten minutes away from the hour, that he in no way deserved these groundless invectives given that the time for him to

5

Guylain was loath to lift the lid of the Zerstor 500's control cabinet. Inexplicably, he felt the unpleasant sensation of the sheet metal vibrating beneath his fingers as he often did, as if the Thing were well and truly alive, juddering with impatience at the thought of beginning a new day. At those times, he went into autopilot. Confining himself to his role as chief operator for which he was paid the generous sum of 1,840 euros each month, including his bonus for having lunch on the premises. He read out every item on the checklist while Brunner went from one checkpoint to the next, twirling around as Guylain named each part. Before releasing the trapdoor that shut off the bottom of the funnel, Guylain glanced over at the gaping mouth, just to check that no intrepid animal had stupidly taken it into its head to venture inside. Rats had become a real problem. The smell drove them wild. The funnel attracted them the way the fragrant lobes of a Venus flytrap lure flies. And it was not unusual to find one that was greedier than the others stuck at the bottom of the hole. When he came across one, Guylain would go and fetch the scoop from the cloakrooms and fish the creature out from the tight spot it had got itself into. And without further ado, it would scamper off towards the back of the plant and vanish from sight. Guylain was not particularly fond of rodents. He was motivated essentially by the wish to deprive the Zerstor of a hunk of meat. It loved meat, he was certain of it, loved those screeching, wriggling little bodies that it crunched like a mere snack when it managed to nab one. And he was convinced that, given the chance, it would gobble up his hands without any qualms. Since Giuseppe's accident, it had been clear to Guylain that rat meat was not always enough to satisfy the Thing.

After priming the pump and flicking the switches

to the ON position, he pressed his thumb on the green button which Brunner dreamed of pushing one day. Guylain counted to five and then released the pressure. You always had to count to five, no more, no less. Less, and the machine wouldn't start; more and you flooded the whole thing. You had to earn your place in hell. High up on his sea captain's bridge, Kowalski did not miss Guylain's slightest movement. The button winked for about ten seconds then shone brightly. At first, nothing happened. The floor barely shuddered when the Thing gave an initial splutter of protest. Its awakening was always laborious. It burped, gasped, sounded reluctant to get going, but once it had gulped down the first mouthful of fuel, the Thing went into action. A dull rumble rose from the ground, followed by a first tremor that assailed Guylain's legs and then ran through his entire body. Soon the thrusts of the powerful diesel motor made the shed shake from floor to ceiling. The earmuffs clamped on Guylain's head barely filtered out the infernal clamour that was unleashed. Down in the belly of the Zerstor, the hammers started up, banging together, metal against metal, in a din that sounded like Armageddon. The blades below chopped frenetically, gleaming in the spent contorting himself in the stinking belly, sweating all the moisture his body contained and submitting to the abuse of a Kowalski more enraged than ever. This morning, the Thing had got off on the right piston. It snapped up and gobbled its first ration of books without the slightest hiccup. Only too happy to crunch something other than air, the hammers were having a field day. Even the noblest spines, the sturdiest bindings, were crushed in seconds. The books disappeared into the Thing's belly in their thousands. The scalding rain relentlessly spewing out of the nozzles around the sides of the tank washed the few flyaway pages that tried to escape down towards the bottom of the funnel. Below, the 600 razor-sharp blades took over, reducing what remained of the sheets of paper into thin strips. The four huge mixers finished the job, converting the whole thing into a thick soup. No trace remained of the books that had lain on the floor only a few minutes earlier. There was nothing but the grey mush that the Thing expelled in the form of great, steaming turds that fell into the vats with a gruesome giant plopping sound. This coarse pulp would be used one day to make other books, some of which would inevitably end up back here,

6

The security guard's hut was an oasis where Guylain liked to take refuge during the lunch hour. Unlike Brunner, who ranted on for the sake of it, Yvon could sit for ages without saying a word, completely engrossed in his reading. His silences were full. Guylain could slip into them as into a warm bath. Sitting with Yvon, his sandwich had less of the after-taste of boiled cardboard that tainted everything he ate since he'd begun working here. Yvon sometimes asked him to give him his cues. 'A sounding board,' he had explained the first time. 'I just need a sound-ing board to bounce my speeches off.' Guylain willingly accepted the part, reciting to the best of his ability lines he barely understood, sometimes changing sex to read the part of Andromaque, Berenice or Iphigenia, while Yvon Grimbert, at the peak of his art, spouted at the top of his voice Pyrrhus, Titus and other Agamemnons of his own composition. Yvon did not eat, contenting himself with his twelve-syllable verses alone, lines which he washed down with the black tea he loved and which he drank by the Thermosful all day long.

The lorry drew up with the long whistle of a tired whale, inches from the lowered barrier. Yvon abandoned Don Rodrigo and Chimene while he glanced up and noted that it was past the cut-off time for deliveries, and then dived back into Act III, Scene 4. The rules stipulated that out of consideration for the local residents, TERN had to cease all activity between 12.00 and 1.30 p.m., a rule that also included halting the comings and goings of the lorries whose job was to feed the Thing. The drivers all knew this and those who arrived after midday ended up having to park in the street until after lunch. Only a few rare reckless souls like this one occasionally tried to bend the rules and blag their way through.

Confident in the power of his thirty-eight-tonne truck, the driver pressed his horn and barked impatiently through his lowered window: 'Hey, I haven't got all day, you know!' Stonewalled by the security guard, the driver got down from the cab and marched angrily over to the hut. 'Hey, you! Are you deaf or what?' Without looking up from the book in front of him, Yvon raised his hand, palm facing forwards, to indicate that for the moment his attention was occupied by something more important than listening to the insults of a truck driver having a hissy fit. Guylain had always seen Yvon apply this principle, which consisted of never stopping mid-sentence, for any reason whatsoever. *Never lose the thread of the Word, kiddo! Go right to the end; glide through the speech until the final full stop releases you!* Tapping on the window in annoyance, the driver said, even more contemptuously, 'When the fuck are you going to lift the barrier?'

A new guy, thought Guylain. Only a newcomer would dare to speak to Yvon Grimbert like that! Slipping a bookmark into his 1953 edition of *The Cid*, Yvon gave Guylain a meaningful look and pointed to the box on the shelf running the length of the hut. It contained years of versifications from suffocating them as surely as a hail of blows to the solar plexus. 'An alexandrine is as direct as a sword,' Yvon had explained to him one day. 'Its job is to hit the target, but it must be used wisely. Don't deliver it like common prose. Recite it standing. Take in plenty of air to give the words impact. Enunciate each syllable with passion and fire; declaim it as if making love, with sonorous hemistichs, broken up by caesuras. The alexandrine demands dedication from an actor. No room for improvisation. You can't cheat with a line of twelve syllables, kiddo.' After so many years of practice, Yvon had become a master in the art of delivery. Drawing himself up to his full height, the security guard came out of his hut:

'*Many a supplier has come to know my wrath,*
But just get here on time and my voice will be soft.
Unload your consignment, and don't look so amazed,
Ended is the torment you caused with this delay.

'*Do try in the future to turn up here on time,*
Legendary patience will not always be mine.
No matter what the hour, no nuisance is so great
As to accept receipt of new freight at this gate.

'Do not drive me crazy, warning is now given,
Within lovely ladies, furies can be hidden.
I remain your servant, yet hardly need to state
That within this precinct, I'm master of your fate.'

By now, the lorry driver was looking seriously worried. All of a sudden, he was no longer watching Yvon Grimbert, lowly security guard, but the all-powerful high priest of the temple. Beneath his greying moustache, Yvon's crimson lips delivered the defiant lines without trembling. The driver ventured a guarded reply and tiptoed back in his cowboy boots to the cab of his Volvo for protection against the avalanche of rhymes. Yvon pursued him. Standing on the running board, he hurled great volleys of verse into the cab while the panic-stricken young driver frantically wound up the window:

'When you are in distress, a juggernaut will serve
To hide your shame and stress until you find
    your nerve.
If you wish to silence the language of the muse,
Do not look so aghast and present your excuse!'

Defeated, his forehead resting on the wheel in an attitude of submission, the driver mumbled a string of garbled words that sounded like an apology. As he made his way back to his glassed-in shelter, Yvon fired off one parting quatrain:

> 'I'm on my way right now to raise up this barrier
> And quietly bring down my level of anger.
> Now move this truck along, empty out its contents
> May the shredder live long, after you are
>   gone hence.'

So saying, Yvon opened the way for the huge vehicle, which snorted a cloud of exhaust fumes. Guylain deserted his poet friend for a moment to supervise the unloading. Still in shock, the driver disgorged his load half onto the platform, half onto the car park. His delivery note stamped, he left, only too happy to see the barrier rise without his having to suffer further assaults from Yvon Grimbert, who was already back in his kingdom of Castile watching out for the Moors by Chimene's side.

7

It was time to clean up – the moment Guylain so loathed. It was no easy task being swallowed whole by the Thing in order to scour its innards. Every evening he had to force himself to go down into the tank, but it was the price he had to pay in order to carry out his mission with complete impunity. Since Kowalski had installed CCTV cameras all over the place, Guylain had not been able to remove samples as easily as before. Giuseppe's accident had given the boss the excuse to equip the entire plant with six state-of-the-art digital cameras, tireless eyes that spied on the workers' every movement all day long.

'To prevent another such tragedy ever happening again,' Fatso had said, his voice full of sorrow. A feigned sorrow that had not deceived Guylain. That bastard Felix Kowalski had never shown an iota of sympathy for the elderly Giuseppe Carminetti, considering him nothing but an unproductive alcoholic, a millstone. Above all he had taken advantage of the unhoped-for opportunity afforded by Giuseppe's accident to carry out what he had always dreamt of doing: spying on his entire little kingdom without having to move his buttocks off the leather armchair he lounged in from dawn till dusk. To hell with Kowalski and his surveillance cameras.

After putting the Zerstor out of action, Guylain would slip down to the base of the funnel. The image of a panic-stricken rat clawing at the stainless steel sides often flashed through his mind at this point. He knew that the Thing was powerless to do any harm – the control unit was switched off, the fuel supply disconnected. But Guylain couldn't help remaining on his guard, alert for the tiniest hint of a tremor, ready to tear himself out of the Thing's clutches if it suddenly felt the urge to make a little snack of him. He released the cylinder housing and slid between the two rows of hammers. He still had to contort himself and crawl almost two metres to reach the lower rollers. He yelled to Brunner to pass him the grease gun through the side hatch. The gangly Brunner was too tall to be able to get inside the machine. It infuriated him not to be able to board the ship, to be forced to remain on the dock and be content with handing Guylain the 32-mm spanner, the oilcan or the hose. Guylain turned on his head lamp. It was here, in the still-warm steel belly, that he gathered the day's harvest. There were a dozen or so pages waiting for him, always in the same spot between the stainless steel wall and the bracket of the last roller spiked with knives – the only place that was out of reach of the water jets. Flyaway pages that had been blown against the partition streaming with water and had landed on this spur of metal which had halted their fatal slide. Giuseppe called them live skins. 'They're the sole survivors of the massacre, kiddo,' he would say, his voice emotional. Guylain hastily half-opened the zip of his boiler suit and slipped the dozen or so sopping pages under his T-shirt. After greasing the bearings one by one and thoroughly washing out the Thing's stomach, he extracted himself from his prison with the day's lucky pages snug and warm against his breast. As he often did, old Kowalski had torn himself out of his armchair to drag his mass of lard to the edge of the pigeon loft. He was tormented by the thought that one of his workers had been out of range of his spyhole for a few minutes. Despite the winking, blinking red lights on his cameras, he would never know what Vignolles got up to in the belly of the Zerstor. And that angelic smile that Guylain bestowed on him every evening on his way to the shower did nothing to reassure him.

Guylain stood under the scalding shower for nearly ten minutes. He was sick of the sludge he wallowed in all day long. He needed to cleanse himself of this muck, wash away his crime between these four yellow-stained walls. He stepped out into the street with the feeling that he had come back from hell. Once on the train taking him back to the fold, he brought out the rescued pages and laid them gently on the blotting paper that would free them of the moisture swelling their fibres. So that the next day, on this same train, the live skins would finally give up the ghost as he released them from their words.

8

Guylain did not read during the return commute. He had neither the energy nor the desire. Nor did he sit on the orange jump seat. After laying the live skins on their blotting paper and putting the folder in his bag, he closed his eyes and allowed himself gradually to come back to life as the carriage rocked his tired body. Twenty peaceful minutes during which life flowed back into him while the ballast streaming past under the train absorbed the day's ill humour.

On exiting the station, Guylain walked up the avenue for nearly a kilometre then disappeared into the maze of pedestrian streets in the city centre. He lived on the third floor of an ancient apartment building at number 48, Allée des Charmilles. His cramped attic studio flat was spartan with its kitchenette from another era, Lilliputian bathroom and worn lino. When it rained, like today, the skylight let in water if there was a wind. In summer, the terracotta tiles greedily drank in the sun's rays and transformed the thirty-six square metres into a furnace. And yet, each evening, Guylain arrived home with the same sense of relief, far from all the world's Brunners and Kowalskis. Before even removing his jacket, Guylain went over and gave a pinch of food to Rouget de Lisle, the goldfish who shared his life, whose bowl stood on the bedside table.

'Sorry I'm a bit late but the 18.48 should have been called the 19.02. I'm knackered. You don't know how lucky you are, my friend. Sometimes I'd give anything to change places with you.'

He had caught himself talking to his fish more and more often. Guylain liked to think that Rouget de Lisle listened to him, suspended in the middle of his sphere, gills flapping, eager to hear about his day. Having a goldfish for a confidant meant expecting nothing from him other than to listen in passive silence, although Guylain sometimes thought he discerned in the stream of bubbles coming from the fish's mouth the beginnings of a reply to his questions. Rouget de Lisle greeted him with a lap of honour then gulped down the food flakes floating on the surface of the water. All the lights on the telephone were winking. As he expected, Giuseppe's voice erupted from the speaker as he listened to his answerphone messages:

'Listen, kiddo!' The old fellow's elated tone at once swept away any shame that overcame Guylain at deceiving his old friend, as he was doing at present. After a long silence, beneath which he could hear the breathing of a Guiseppe almost fainting with emotion, the gravelly voice resumed:

'Albert's just called. We've got one! Call me as soon as you get in.' The command brooked no evasion. Giuseppe picked up before the end of the first ring. Guylain smiled. The old boy was waiting for his call. He pictured him bundled up in the light-green blanket he always had wrapped around him, the telephone resting on what remained of his legs, his hand clenching the receiver.

'How many is it now, Giuseppe?'

'*Sette cento cinquantanove!*'

His mother tongue rose to the surface when he was overcome with anger or an immense joy, as he was now. Seven hundred and fifty-nine – that took them up to where? wondered Guylain. Above the ankles? Mid-calf?

'No, I meant how long since the last one?' fibbed Guylain, who remembered perfectly well the date circled in red on the wall calendar hanging next to the fridge.

'Three months and seventeen days. It was the twenty-second of November last year. That time it had been one of his contacts who works at the waste recycling centre in Livry-Gargan who'd found it. It was sitting on top of the pile in the waste-paper skip. It was the colour that had attracted his attention. He said it was a good thing I'd taken a photo to give to all the lads. That's how he recognized it: from the colour. There aren't any other books like it, he said. It's exactly the same as the colour of the old missals when he was a choirboy. Jesus, just think! What's more, it's in excellent condition, he says, apart from a faint grease stain on the top right-hand corner of the back cover.'

Guylain congratulated himself once again for having chosen the second-hand bookseller as an ally in carrying out his campaign of deceit, even though he feared that one day Albert, the legendary *bouquiniste* of Quai de la Tournelle, famous for his mischievous humour, would arouse the old boy's suspicions by saying too much. *Make a grease stain on the back of the book* – Guylain made a mental note. 'Tomorrow, Giuseppe. I'll go and pick it up tomorrow, I promise. I'm too worn out tonight, and anyway, it's a bit late to catch the last train back. Tomorrow's Saturday and I'll have plenty of time.'

'All right, kiddo, tomorrow. In any case, Albert's holding on to it. He's expecting you.'

Guylain nibbled gingerly at a plate of rice. Lying, over and over again. He fell asleep watching Rouget de Lisle digest his food. On the TV, a reporter was talking about a revolution in a far-off country and about a population being wiped out.

victim.' Alcohol, that's what had done for Giuseppe, Guylain was convinced. The army of lawyers and experts hired by TERN had simply pointed the finger without looking any further for the true causes of that whole shambolic incident. Those vultures only just stopped short of billing him for the tattered boiler suit and the forty-five minutes lost production time while the Zerstor was halted. Forty-five brief minutes, not a minute more; just the time it took for the firemen to free Giuseppe, who was howling with pain and writhing at the bottom of the tank like a man condemned, surrounded by books that were drinking his blood, his entire mind sucked into the two wells of suffering that had taken the place of his legs. He had just replaced one of the lateral nozzles and was about to climb out of the funnel when the Thing had devoured his lower limbs, right up to his mid-thighs. The ambulance doors were barely shut before Kowalski himself started the machine up again while Guylain puked his guts out, clutching the toilet bowl with both hands. That bastard had set the machine in motion with Giuseppe's screams still echoing through the works. Guylain had not forgiven Fatso for this. Starting up again with the sole aim of finishing what had been begun, in other words reducing the contents of a thirty-eight-tonne tipper to a paste. Into the guts of the Zerstor it all went, where it was mixed with the formless pulp that was all that remained of chief operator Carminetti's pins. The show must go on and God rest his legs!

Alcohol did not explain everything. Guylain had believed Giuseppe when he'd sworn that he'd carried out the safety procedures, that, of course, that day he'd knocked back his habitual little tipple, as he did every God-given day, but that he would never have gone down into the tank without taking the usual safety precautions. Guylain knew Giuseppe and his general mistrust of the Thing. 'Beware of it, kiddo! It's vicious and could very well do to us one day what it does to the rats!' he was always saying. He too had noticed. They had never really discussed the rat problem. Not easy to raise things that defied reason. Each knew that the other knew, that was all. Just once, Giuseppe had had a word with Kowalski about it. That had been a long time before the disaster. After coming across an umpteenth victim one morning, Giuseppe had gone to see Fatso to tell him of his concerns, but nothing had happened as a result. The boss must have taken the piss out of him as he always did and sent him packing with his customary charm, presumed Guylain. Giuseppe had come out of the office as white as a sheet, looking solemn. Guylain hadn't said anything. He still regretted it. Perhaps if he had backed Giuseppe up, the company would have investigated the matter properly and tried to find an explanation for the presence of mutilated rats in the vat stuck to the Zerstor 500's arse first thing in the morning, whereas it had been empty the previous evening. Guylain had conducted his own investigation, following every possible lead, eliminating them one by one until there was only one plausible explanation, the most difficult to accept, the most improbable and yet the only one that held water. In other words, the Thing was possibly more than just a machine, sometimes starting up of its own accord in the middle of the night when one of those wretched rodents came scurrying around in its craw.

One year after the accident, and following recurrent problems with power cuts, a complete overhaul of the Zerstor's controls revealed a problem with the circuit-breaker lever. A faulty switch was no longer doing its job properly and allowed the current to flow at whim, even when the lever was in the OFF position. After that, all the safety mechanisms were reinforced, most of them even doubled, to ensure that such a tragedy would never occur again. Furthermore, management had agreed that perhaps Carminetti, former chief operator of the Zerstor 500, had been the victim of an unfortunate incident leading to the sudden resumption of operations while he inopportunely happened to be in the tank. Consequently, Giuseppe, who had already come to terms with the idea of having to survive on minimum benefits, had ended up being compensated to the tune of 176,000 euros for the loss sustained. '88,000 euros per leg!' Giuseppe had announced tearfully over the phone. It wasn't so much the money but rather the fact that they had finally accepted the word of a wino that had made Giuseppe truly happy that day, Guylain thought. He had always wondered on what basis the experts calculated the value of a death, a trauma or a limb, as in Giuseppe's case. Why 88,000 and not 87,000 or 89,000? Did they take the length of the leg into

'A Butterfly 750, kiddo! Amazing, not even twelve kilos! And the colour, look at the colour. Mauve. I chose it just for the colour. What do you think?' Guylain had not been able to suppress a smile. Listening to him, it almost made him want to go and have his legs gobbled up by the first Zerstor he came across, just for the pleasure of having a nice new wheelchair too. And then Giuseppe had begun to say worrying things, talking of 'getting them back'. 'When I've got them back, things'll be better. Just you wait, kiddo', he'd say each time Guylain visited, his eyes bright with hope. At first Guylain told himself that perhaps the Thing had devoured a bit more than Giuseppe's legs and partially destroyed his mind in the process. It wasn't the alcohol talking – the old boy had become a teetotaller overnight. Now that he was away from the plant, he no longer drank. Guylain had asked him exactly what 'them' were and what he meant by 'when I've got them back', even though of course he had his own ideas on the subject. Giuseppe would then clam up, promising to tell him everything when he was ready. For as long as he lived, Guylain would remember his friend's radiant face when he'd opened the door to him a few weeks later, clutching the precious book. Giuseppe had shat into the vats by the Thing on that cursed day in April 2002. The start of a long journey, to end up in this inconsequential book and in the 1,299 others made with this unique paper pulp. Guylain stood there dumbfounded. The old fellow had found his legs.

bookshops up and down the country to strip them of the sought-after book, Giuseppe had had the brainwave of paying a visit to the second-hand booksellers on the banks of the Seine. One fine day, the old boy and his wheelchair had turned up on their patch and pirouetted from one stall to the next telling them his story and explaining how he, Giuseppe Carminetti, former chief operator of the TERN treatment and recycling company, ex-alcoholic and ex-biped, was going to do his utmost to recover the books that contained what was left of his pins. He had given each of them his card, with the quirky book title written on the back. They had been moved by his quest. Each bookstall owner had immediately roped in his own network to hunt down the Holy Grail. Not a weekend went by without Guylain paying a visit to the booksellers on the riverbank to act as courier and bring the fruits of the harvest to Giuseppe. He had enjoyed those strolls, contemplating the *bateaux-mouches* packed with tourists gliding lazily through the Seine's silvery waters. It was good to be aware that there was another world outside TERN, a world where books were allowed to end their lives snugly arranged inside the green booths lining the parapets, growing

JEAN-PAUL DIDIERLAURENT

old to the pulse of the great river watched over by the towers of Notre Dame.

The 500 mark had been reached less than a year and a half after the beginning of this mad venture, and the 700 one three years later. And then the inevitable happened. The source eventually dried up and the counter stayed stuck at 746. Giuseppe then sank into a profound state of gloom. All these months, the quest had been his main reason for living. It gave him the strength to cope with the columns of ants that attacked his phantom limbs night after night and helped him to put up with the pitying looks people showered on him when he roamed the streets in his Butterfly. Almost overnight, Giuseppe had given up. For nearly a year, Guylain had battled to keep up the old boy's morale, visiting him once or twice a week. After rolling up the blinds to let the light in and opening the windows to get some fresh air into the stale-smelling apartment, he would sit down opposite him and gently take his friend's hands, two warm dying birds that meekly allowed themselves to be caught. Then, chatting about this and that, he would steer Giuseppe into the bathroom. He bathed and rubbed down his friend's battered body, shaved the straggling bristles on his cheeks and chin and combed his thick locks. Next, Guylain washed the dirty dishes mouldering in the sink and picked up the clothes scattered over the floor throughout the apartment. He never left without explaining to Giuseppe that he had to hang in there, that all was not lost, that time acted on books like ice on buried stones and that sooner or later they would surface. But all his efforts to coax the old boy out of his sluggish state were to no avail. Only new finds could rekindle the fire in Giuseppe's eyes.

How the idea of contacting Jean-Eude Freyssinet had come to him, Guylain couldn't say. On the other hand, it was strange that it hadn't occurred to anyone else, not even to Giuseppe, to contact the author of *Gardens and Kitchen Gardens of Bygone Days* directly. He'd had no trouble tracking down the illustrious writer's telephone number and Madame Freyssinet had answered on the fifth ring. She informed him in a quavering voice that her Jean-Eude had passed on a few years ago, halfway through writing his second book, an essay on *Cucurbitaceae* and other dicotyledons of central Europe. Without beating about the bush, Guylain had explained to the widow that within the unsold slurry-coloured copies that she had kept in memory of her departed there was something more than her husband's spiritual legacy. She immediately suggested that she only needed to keep a few copies and offered to let him have the rest of her collection, which represented around a hundred pristine copies of *Gardens and Kitchen Gardens of Bygone Days*. Giving them to Giuseppe all at once would have been a grave mistake, Guylain knew. It was the search that mattered. The Freyssinet collection had to be distilled sparingly, at a rate of three or four a year, never more. Just enough to bring a glimmer to the old boy's eyes and keep the hunter on the alert.

During the years of plenty, the famous Albert had become the self-appointed spokesman for the *bouquinistes*. His cheeky humour was a huge hit with the tourists he snared in his banter like a spider catching flies in its web. And it was naturally to him that Guylain turned to put his scheme into action. It worked like a dream. When he felt the time had come – in other words, when the old boy was showing fresh signs of losing hope and sinking into despondency – Guylain would give Albert the go-ahead. The bookseller would then call Giuseppe,

11

Giuseppe lived on the ground floor of a brand-new apartment block, less than ten minutes away. Guylain didn't even need to ring the bell – Giuseppe yelled at him to come in from the kitchen where he had been watching out for him, his face pressed to the window. The place smelled clean. Guylain took his shoes off in the hall and, following an unchanging ritual, put on Giuseppe's old slippers, two orphaned slippers which always seemed happy to feel two feet in them again. The bookshelves ate up an entire wall of the living room. The 758 copies of *Gardens and Kitchen Gardens of Bygone Days* by

Jean-Eude Freyssinet sat cover to cover in neat rows on the mahogany planks, their slurry-green spines exposed. Giuseppe's babies. He had a special way of caressing their edges with his fingertips as he passed them, and he took particular care to dust them regularly. They were the flesh of his flesh. He had given them his blood and more. And it mattered little that it happened to be the unimportant work of a Jean-Wotsit-Thingummyjig and not the winner of that year's Goncourt. You can't choose your children's looks. The poignant emptiness of the shelves above them were a daily reminder of that part of himself that had not yet returned to the fold. Anxious and unable to contain himself a moment longer, Giuseppe gripped Guylain's arm.

'Well?'

Not wanting to prolong his agony, Guylain put the book in his hands. Giuseppe turned it over and over, examined it in the light, checked the ISBN, the dates and printing numbers, leafed through it, assessed the paper quality with his fingertips, sniffed it and caressed the pages with the palm of his hand. Only then did he hug it to his chest with a smile. Each time, Guylain marvelled at the moving sight of his tormented face bursting into a huge, radiant took him by surprise. He had eaten nothing at lunchtime. And Giuseppe knew him well enough to know that he had eaten nothing that day other than a handful of cereal washed down by a mug of scalding tea. The old boy's beady little eyes read all that in his silence. 'I've made some food for you.' His peremptory tone left Guylain no option but to accept the invitation. When Giuseppe cooked, it was the whole of Italy that landed on your plate. After an anchovy paste with a bundle of cabled *grissini*, washed down with a glass of Prosecco, came a heaped plate of melon with *prosciutto crudo* accompanied by a red Lacryma Christi. Giuseppe loved reminding him that getting drunk on Christ's tears was the best thing that could happen to a Christian. Guylain was surprised to find that for a while he was able to forget the flavour of boiled cardboard that coated his taste buds. The dessert, comprising a dish of crunchy almond *amaretti* with a glass of home-made *limoncello*, chilled to perfection, was sheer bliss. They chatted idly and solved all the world's problems. The Thing had made them very close, a closeness that only trench warfare is capable of forging between soldiers who have shared the same shell hole. It was nearly one o'clock in the morning when Guylain took his leave of Giuseppe. The ten-minute walk through the freezing night was not enough to sober him up. He just took the time to remove his shoes and say goodnight to Rouget de Lisle before collapsing fully clothed on his bed, drunk with wine and exhaustion.

12

The mobile phone set to wake him at 5.30 vibrated on the bedside table. Beneath the water's undulating surface, Rouget de Lisle's protruding eyes stared at him from his bowl. Monday. Where had Sunday gone? Got up too late, went to bed too early. A day without. Without desire, without hunger, without thirst, without even a memory.

Rouget and he had spent their day going round in circles, the fish in his bowl, and he in his studio flat, already filled with dread at the thought of Monday. Guylain sprinkled a pinch of food on the water and forced himself to eat the handful of cereal he'd poured into his bowl. He brushed his teeth between two sips of tea, pulled on his clothes and grabbed the leather briefcase, then tore down the three flights of stairs into the cold outside, fully awake by now.

As he walked down the avenue to the station, Guylain counted the lamp posts. Counting was the best way he had found to stop himself from thinking about the rest. He counted anything and everything. One day the manholes, another the parked cars, the dustbins or entrances to buildings. The road had no more secrets from him. He sometimes even counted his own steps. Taking refuge in this pointless counting exercise stopped him thinking of those other numbers, all those tonnages that old Kowalski bawled from his watchtower on peak delivery days.

Every day at the same time, when Guylain reached house number 154, he saw the old-man-in-slippers-and-pyjamas-under-his-raincoat desperately trying to coax his dog, an anaemic poodle with a tatty coat, to pee. And as always, the old fellow, his rapt gaze riveted on his beloved, was urging the dog, whose name was Balthus, to empty his bladder against the semblance of a plane tree struggling to survive by the roadside. Guylain never failed to greet the old-man-in-slippers-and-pyjamas-under-his-raincoat and to egg on Balthus in his urinary peregrinations with a friendly pat. He counted another eighteen lamp posts before reaching the station.

Standing on the white line, Guylain was floating in a state of drowsiness when he felt someone tugging his sleeve. He turned round. They had crept up silently behind him. Two little old biddies who were literally devouring him with their eyes. Their permed hair had the same purplish hue as Giuseppe's Butterfly 750. The mauve rinses were not unfamiliar to him. He had the feeling he had already seen these ladies on the train several times before. The one who was standing furthest back nudged the other: 'Go on, Monique, you do the talking.'

Monique didn't dare. She kneaded her hands, not knowing what to do with them, cleared her throat, kept saying, 'Yes, yes', 'All right', 'Stop it, Josette', or 'I'm going to'. Guylain almost felt like reassuring Monique, telling her it was OK, that everything would be fine, that striking up a conversation was the hardest bit and afterwards the words would come all by themselves, that there was no need to be afraid. Except that he had no idea what these good ladies wanted from him, other than the obvious fact that they wanted to talk to him. Gripping her handbag as if it were a lifebelt, Monique finally took the plunge: 'It's that we wanted to tell you that we really like what you do.'

'What do you mean, what I do?' asked Guylain incredulously.

'Well, when you read on the train in the morning and all that. We love it, and it does us no end of good.'

'Thank you, that's very kind of you, but you know, it's not much, just a few odd pages.'

'Exactly. So Josette and I would like to ask you something, if we may. Of course, we'd understand if you couldn't, but we'd be so thrilled if you said yes. It would make us so happy, and it wouldn't take up much of your time, and it would be whenever's convenient for you, depending on when you're free. We really don't want to be a bother.'

Guylain almost wished the one called Monique would go back to silently kneading her hands.

'I'm sorry, but what do you mean exactly by "make you so happy"?'

'Well, actually, we'd like you to come to our home and read to us from time to time.'

She exhaled the end of her sentence in a sigh, which made the last words barely audible. Guylain couldn't help staring blissfully at these two octogenarian fans who were demanding him exclusively for themselves. Touched by this unusual request, he stammered the beginnings of a reply: 'Um, I mean . . .'

'But,' Monique broke in, 'I should tell you that Thursday's no good because there's rummy, though any other day would be fine. Except Sundays, of course, because of the families.'

'Hold on, I only read odd bits and pieces, random pages that have no connection with each other. I don't read entire books.'

'No, we know that! It doesn't worry us. Quite the opposite! That's even better – it's less monotonous and then at least if the extract is boring, we know it won't go on for more than a page. Josette and I have been coming to listen to you on the train every Monday and Thursday morning for nearly a year now. It's a bit early for us but it doesn't matter, it gets us out. And besides, as it's market day, we kill two birds with one stone.'

They were sweet, these two little old dears muffled up in their beige coats, both hanging on to his every word. Guylain had a sudden urge to give in to their madness, to export his live skins to somewhere other than this gloomy carriage which he rode every day.

'But where do you live?'

To their ears his question sounded like a firm and definite yes. Elated, the two women congratulated each other and jumped up and down on the spot. As the one called Monique put her card in Guylain's hand, the other whispered in her ear, 'I told you he was nice.' The visiting card stated the name and address in the middle of a bed of pastel flowers. Mesdemoiselles Monique and Josette Delacôte, 7 bis, Impasse de la Butte, 93220 Gagny. A line had been neatly crossed out with a ballpoint pen. Guylain presumed that Monique and Josette were sisters. Impasse de la Butte – that was up the hill, a good half hour's walk from his place.

'We've already discussed it. If you agree to come, we'll pay the return taxi fare. It'll be easier for you and less tiring.'

Guylain told himself that the Delacôte sisters must have been plotting this for a good while before approaching him. 'Look, I don't mind giving it a go, but I don't want you to consider this a long-term commitment. Let's get that clear, shall we? I'm happy to give it a try, but I want to be able to stop at any time.'

'Oh! Josette and I fully understand, don't we, Josette? And which day could you come?'

What was he getting himself into? On weekday evenings, Guylain was too exhausted to be able to do anything. 'I'm only free on Saturdays. Preferably late morning.'

'OK for Saturdays, but at around ten thirty because we have lunch at half past eleven.'

As the train pulled into the station, they finalized arrangements for him to come at 10.30 the following Saturday. Sitting on his folding seat, Guylain began reading the first live skin of the day, a recipe for farmhouse vegetable soup, watched eagerly by the delighted Delacôte sisters, who had sat themselves on the nearest seat, better to drink in his words.

13

From Monday to Friday, Guylain's brain was numb from work. In the run-up to the Paris Book Fair in April, the stream of lorries swelled considerably. The bumper crop of autumn books and the prosperous prize season were long over. Space had to be made, the shelves emptied of all the unsold books. The newcomers were pushing the oldest towards the exit, assisted by the bulldozer's blade. From dawn to dusk, they had to flatten again and again that damned mountain that continually rose up from the works floor. The containers filled at a rate of one every twenty minutes. They no longer even halted the Zerstor when they replaced the vats filled with pulp. 'Wastes too much time,' Kowalski had barked at the beginning of the week. 'It slows things down too much and we lose containers with all the messing around.' So they had to wade around in the sludge each time they changed the vats and feel the brunt, without flinching, of the Thing's foul-smelling farts right in their faces as they stood behind it. And when it was finally time to go home, Guylain still had to put up with Kowalski, who came out to bawl the day's tonnage proudly at them from up on his gangway. For Fatso, the only thing that mattered was the curve, that inconsequential red line with tonnes on the X-axis and euros on the Y-axis, which looked like a great blood-coloured gash across the nineteen-inch screen on his desk.

The weekend arrived like a haven in which to deposit all the fatigue built up during the week. Monique and Josette Delacôte were expecting him. The taxi ordered fifteen minutes earlier appeared at the top of the road and drew up at his feet.

Guylain clambered inside and gave the address to the driver, who gave an authoritative jerk of the steering wheel and joined the heavy Saturday morning traffic. Less than ten minutes later, the car turned onto a wide gravel drive. As they drove through the gate, Guylain was able to read the inscription in gilt lettering on the gleaming plate. 'Magnolia Court.' He immediately recalled the two words that had been crossed out on the Delacôte sisters' visiting card. Catching sight of the imposing building surrounded by gardens, Guylain was unable to suppress a gasp of surprise. From the start, he had been expecting a little suburban house. As the taxi drove the last few metres, he remembered the elderly lady's words: *We have lunch at half past eleven. Thursday's no good because there's rummy. Except Sundays, of course, because of the families.* It all made sense at the sight of the many silhouettes at the windows. He realized then that when she'd said 'we' she hadn't meant just the two sisters. The sound of the gravel crunching under the wheels of the taxi died away as he walked with a hesitant step towards the house.

Monique came trotting out to meet him, with Josette close behind like her shadow. They were primped and preened as for their first ball. 'We were afraid you'd changed your mind at the last minute and that you weren't coming. Everyone's dying to see you, you know.'

Guylain choked back his anxiety. How many people was 'everyone'? Panic-stricken, he imagined a sea of purple rinses. He wished momentarily that he'd stayed under his duvet watching Rouget de Lisle blowing bubbles.

'Come on, we'll introduce you. By the way, we don't even know your name.'

'Guylain. Guylain Vignolles.'

'Oh, Guylain, that's a pretty name. Very pretty, isn't it, Josette?' Guylain told himself he could have been called Gérard, Anicet or Houcine and it would not have made a jot of difference to the way Josette devoured him with her eyes. He walked into Magnolia Court flanked by the two sisters hanging on his arms. In the spacious lobby there were half a dozen old folk slumped on seats, snoozing. The building looked new. Impersonal, functional and sterile were the three words that came to mind as Guylain discovered the place. The tap-tapping of walking sticks must echo as in a crypt, he thought with a shudder. It smelled of nothing, not even death.

'This way,' whispered Monique, steering him

towards the dining room. 'You'll have to speak in a loud voice, of course.'

The room was packed. Around twenty men and women were herded in there, each older than the other. When he stepped through the door, they X-rayed him from head to foot. The staff were among them, recognizable not only by their youthful age but by their pink uniforms. The tables had been pushed back against the walls to make space. Guylain stared nervously at the armchair in the centre of the room, whose armrests invited him to be seated.

14

'I am delighted to introduce Mr Guylain Gignolle, who is honouring us with his presence today and will kindly read to us. Please give him a warm welcome.'

Guylain gratified Monique with an indulgent smile for mangling his name and greeted the gathering with a curt nod. Mademoiselle Delacôte number two fluttered her eyelids at him in a flash of pearly salmon-pink eyeshadow and jerked her chin at the armchair inviting him to be seated. Like a robot, Guylain walked across the room with a gait he intended to be casual but which was stilted and unsteady due to the huge bag he was carrying. The room was as hot as a pizza oven, minus the aroma. Guylain sat down on the padded velvet Louis-something-or-other armchair and took the little bundle of loose pages from his satchel. Then, with all eyes staring at him through their cataracts or incipient cataracts, he began reading the first live skin:

'Ilsa watched the fly. The dog gazed, fascinated, at the insect as it continually buzzed in and out of the man's gaping mouth. It was always the same little game. The fly rose up into the air for a moment, with that funny way flies have of flying and which irritated Ilsa, veering off at right angles as if imprisoned in an invisible cube and then returning to its starting point. It was a plump bluebottle, its shiny blue abdomen swollen to bursting with hundreds of eggs that were just waiting to hatch as soon as they were deposited in the midst of all that dead meat. The dog had never noticed just how interesting a fly could be. She usually just chased them by moving her head, seeing them simply as little black specks that buzzed through the air. Her jaws often snapped shut on thin air. When *winter came, the flies vanished as if by magic, leaving behind them the occasional desiccated corpse on the windowsill. In winter, the dog forgot about flies until the following summer.*

'*The fly landed on the man's lower lip, marched up and down like a soldier patrolling the battlements, then went in and wandered over the purple tongue. It vanished completely from Ilsa's sight as it disappeared into the dark, moist depths to go and lay its new clutch of eggs in the cold flesh. From time to time, the fly abandoned the corpse to go and settle on the pot of jam sitting on the table. The dog could see its tiny proboscis attach itself to the translucent surface of the redcurrant jelly. The smell of coffee still hung in the air, heavy and sweet. When the bowl had shattered, it left a pretty star-shaped puddle . . .*'

A muted purring reached Guylain's ears from the third row where a dear lady, her head lolling back and her mouth wide open, seemed to be inviting the fly to come and visit her next. The rest of the audience, sitting stock-still, waited in reverent silence to hear more. Beaming with delight, Monique gave him the thumbs up. As he turned the page over to read the other side, a lady bleated a question: 'But do we know what this man died of?' This was the cue for others to pipe up. Questions and suppositions rained down from all sides.

'From an attack; it's bound to be an attack.'

'What kind of attack? And why would it be an attack, can you tell us that, André?' sniped a sickly-looking lady.

Guylain did not know what André had done or not done to this fury in a sky-blue quilted dressing gown, but the reply had the sting of a hard slap.

'How on earth would I know? An aneurysmal rupture or a heart attack. Some sort of attack,' mumbled the old fellow.

'Ye-es, but why doesn't his wife call an ambulance?' asked another.

'What wife? It's not his wife, it's his dog. Lisa, her name is,' chipped in an old man wearing a baseball hat.

'Lisa's no name for a dog.'

'Why not? Look at Germaine – she called her canary Roger, like her late husband.' The Germaine in question squirmed in her chair with embarrassment.

'I thought it was the fly that was called Lisa, I

did,' stuttered an old bod dressed in black from head to toe.

'Please, please, maybe we could let Monsieur Gignal read us the next bit, which I'm sure will tell us more,' cut in Monique authoritatively.

Clearly, thought Guylain, Mademoiselle Delacôte number one had the art of truncating his name every time she opened her mouth. Taking advantage of the brief lull, he jumped into the breach of silence that she had opened up to carry on reading:

'. . . and splattered the chair legs and the man's socks. But beneath the fragrant aroma rising from the floor, Ilsa detected another much headier smell. It was the lingering odour of blood. It was everywhere, imbuing every molecule of air that the dog breathed, a prisoner like her of the tiny enclosed space. Ilsa could not get away from it. This smell was driving her crazy. The bright red pool had rapidly spread on the Formica top, first surrounding the pot of jam and then reaching the edge of the table and dripping slowly onto the floor. Litres of blood had gushed out in a beautiful scarlet geyser through the tiny bullet hole . . .'

'Ha! You see, André, it wasn't an attack.'
'Shh!'

'. . . *in the man's temple. When the shot rang out, Ilsa curled up into a tight ball, her heart pounding wildly. She was unable to take her eyes off the smoking muzzle of the gun which had clattered onto the wooden floor. The man was slumped forward onto the table like a sandbag, his head turned towards her, his wide-open eyes staring. For three days now, his eyelids had not blinked. Once again, the dog scrambled up the narrow staircase to the door, which its paws had scratched with all the energy of despair, achieving nothing but chipping the varnish. Ilsa gulped at the warm, moisture-laden air surging through the keyhole. It had a stale, briny tang.*'*

End of the first sheet. Usually, when he read on the train in the mornings, Guylain immediately went on to the next page, but today – was it their burning gaze or the depth of the silence that had fallen? – he paused and looked up. Every single person was staring at him, even the lady-who-snored-with-her-head-thrown-back who was back among them. He had the sense that there were too many questions left hanging in the air, too many mysteries that needed resolving, or at least containing.

'So it wasn't an attack,' rapped out the fat woman

full of venom, who above all sounded thrilled to have caught André out. To her left, a woman raised her hand. Monique gave her a curt nod, permitting her to speak.

'Is it a suicide?'

'Well, it certainly looks like it,' he was surprised to hear himself answer in a conciliatory tone.

'I bet he did it with a .45,' stated a short, tubby man with a rasping voice.

'Nah, I reckon it was a .22. It says there was a tiny hole,' piped up another.

'And why wouldn't it be a rifle?' mumbled an elderly lady hunched in her wheelchair.

'Come on, Madame Ramier, how can a person shoot themselves in the temple with a rifle?'

'Or it's a murder, but I don't think so,' suggested a little old man, looking dubious.

'But where is this happening?' asked the one called André.

'Yes, where is it happening? And why did the man do it?' added an old dear in a worried tone.

'Well, *I* think it's in a farmhouse in the middle of the woods.'

'And why not an apartment in the city? It's not unheard of. Every year they find people who've been dead for days, sometimes weeks, even though there were neighbours all around them.'

'Well, *I* say that it's on a boat. A sailing ship or a little yacht. The fellow's set sail for the open seas with his dog before blowing his brains out. It says so: it talks about moisture-laden air with a stale, briny tang.'

Monique, who seemed embarrassed by the turn things had taken, went over to Guylain to whisper some advice.

'Monsieur Vignal, it might be a good idea to carry on and start the second reading. Time's getting on.'

'You are right, Monette.'

'No, I'm Monique.'

Monique's thing must be contagious, thought Guylain. 'Sorry, Monique.'

He regretted to say that although their questions were justified, they needed to move on and leave the corpse, the fly and the dog to carry on roaming the seas, the woods or Montmartre if they preferred. A little old lady in the front row who had been fidgeting for a good five minutes raised her hand.

'Yes, Gisèle?' asked Monique.

'May I be excused?'

'Of course you may, Gisèle.'

Guylain witnessed the flight of half a dozen old biddies amid a tapping of sticks and a scraping of chairs. The whole lot of them scurried, wheeled themselves or hobbled off in the direction of the toilets.

Monique signalled to him that it was getting late and that he should start a new reading. He selected a new live skin at random from the pile at his feet.

'For nearly ten minutes, Yvonne Pinchard's voice had been pouring into the priest's ear. The little latticework shutter behind which Father Duchaussoy was ensconced was barely able to filter the stream of whispered words that gushed into the confessional in a torrent of syllables. The woman's whining tone conveyed great outbursts of repentance. From time to time, the priest murmured a discreet "yes" to encourage her. After several decades of priesthood, he excelled in that art which consists of inviting people to continue without ever interrupting them. Blowing gently on the embers, rekindling the transgression in order to spark penitence. Not putting the semblance of forgiveness in their path. No, let them go through with it to the end, until at last they crumple of their own accord under

the burden of remorse. Despite the rapid pace of her confession, it took Yvonne Pinchard a good five minutes more to pour out her soul. Leaning against the partition, the man of the Church collected an umpteenth yawn in his hands while his stomach rumbled in protest. The elderly priest was hungry. Since the early years of his priesthood, he had grown accustomed to dining frugally on confession nights – a salad followed by fresh fruit was often sufficient. Not stuffing himself unreasonably and saving room for all the rest. The weight of sins was not a hollow expression, oh no. Two hours of penitential vigil could nourish you and satiate your body just as much as a communion banquet. A sink waste pipe – that was what he was when he found himself shut up with God in that tiny cubbyhole. No more and no less than one of those huge waste pipes that collected all the filth of the Earth in their metal bowl. People knelt, placed their dirty little souls under his nose just as they would hold their mud-caked shoes under the kitchen tap. A quick absolution and they were done. They left with the light tread of the pure. Then he would leave the church with a laboured step, his head nauseous with the filth that had seeped into his ears. But now, inured over the years, he heard confession without joy, without sadness either, contenting himself with plunging into the semi-torpor inevitably induced in him by the cosy atmosphere of the confessional.'

Guylain quickly grabbed a third sheet before the avalanche of questions that was bound to follow if he waited too long. The clock over the double door already showed 11.15.

'The hitchhiker had told him her name was Gina.

John had desperately tried to catch the eye of the young woman hidden behind a huge pair of sunglasses. For the umpteenth—'

'Monsieur Vagnol, I think Madame Lignon wants to ask you something,' interrupted Monique.

The elderly lady in question was a tall, thin woman who sat stiff as a ramrod beside Monique. A Giacometti sculpture in flesh and bone, thought Guylain.

'No problem, carry on reading.'

'Go on, Huguette,' encouraged Delacôte number one.

'Well, I was a primary school teacher for nearly forty years and I always loved those reading aloud exercises. I'd be delighted to read a page.'

'With the greatest of pleasure. Huguette, is that right? Come and make yourself comfortable, Huguette.'

She clawed the page from his fingers and she seated herself in the armchair. The steel-rimmed spectacles balanced on her nose made her look like a retired schoolmarm, which was very fitting, thought Guylain, because that's what she was. The class immediately fell silent. Her voice was surprisingly clear except for a slight tremor, probably due to her emotion:

'*The hitchhiker had told him her name was Gina.*

John had desperately tried to catch the eye of the young woman hidden behind a huge pair of sunglasses. For the umpteenth time since he had picked her up, Gina crossed her legs, shapely legs that seemed to go on forever. The silky rustle of her nylon stockings was torture.'

Guylain jumped. That last sentence read by Huguette Lignon made him break out in a cold sweat. He instantly grasped that there was going to be a little problem. Since he had been rescuing live skins from the belly of the Zerstor, he had never taken the trouble to glance at them beforehand, preferring to deliver his reading without knowing the content in advance. In all these years, never until this moment had he come across the kind of excerpt that Huguette was reading, a Huguette in seventh heaven who was trying her utmost to find the right tone. So far she did not seem to have realized that she was heading down a slippery slope. Nor for that matter had the audience, who sat spellbound.

'*As he forced himself to keep his eyes on the road ahead, the woman asked him for a light. Generally, he would not allow anyone to smoke inside his truck, but he found himself proffering her his lighter. She grasped his wrist in both hands and brought the flame close to the Chesterfield wedged between her lips, two full lips emphasized with a touch of gloss. She leaned forward towards the ashtray, brushing John's muscular biceps with her nipple as she did so. John shivered at the contact with her delightfully firm breast.*'

Christ! It was what he feared. They were heading for disaster if he didn't step in quickly. He had to stop this before John and Gina ended up lying stark naked on the bunk exchanging bodily fluids. And at this rate, it was likely to happen before the end of page two.

'Huguette, I think it might be better to—'

'Hush!' was the unanimous response of the audience, who hadn't missed a crumb of the story, making it plain to Guylain that any intervention on his part would be most unwelcome. He attracted Monique's attention by clicking his fingers but she was utterly mesmerized. As for her little sister, leaning against the wall, her eyes closed, she was lapping up the increasingly clear and less and less quavering voice of Huguette, who ploughed ahead without deviating from her course.

'*Filled with a growing desire, the truck driver soon felt a little too constricted in his tight jeans. This woman was the devil, a desirable devil who flung her head back each time she exhaled, blowing out her cigarette smoke towards the ceiling light, arching her hips and thrusting her breasts forward. She removed her sunglasses, revealing two vivid blue eyes. Resting her elbow on the door, she turned towards John and partially opened her legs in a lascivious pose. Then, unable to control himself, he brought the thirty-eight-*

*tonne vehicle to an abrupt halt on the hard shoulder,
sending up a huge cloud of dust, and threw himself
on the woman, who offered herself to him without
any resistance. As he ripped off her lace panties, he
tasted those lips parted to receive him. Gina slid an
expert hand inside John's trousers, seeking his turgescent cock.'*

A car hooting outside brought everyone back
down to earth again. On the gravelled drive, the taxi
was flashing its lights impatiently. A few of the residents came over to thank Guylain warmly for his
visit, saying they were sorry it had been so brief.
There was colour in their cheeks, a sparkle in their
eyes. Huguette's reading seemed to have brought a
bit of life back to Magnolia Court. One dear old
soul, her napkin already around her neck for lunch,
asked anyone who happened to be listening what
'turgescent' meant. Guylain dashed off, not without
promising to come back the following Saturday.
He had not felt so alive for a long time.

15

The memory stick came into Guylain Vignolles's life through pure chance. He could so easily not have seen it, or even quite simply ignored it. It might also have ended up in other hands, met a different fate. The fact is that early one chilly March morning, it jumped out of the folding seat as he lowered it. A little plastic thing barely the size of a domino which bounced across the floor of the compartment and came to a halt between his feet. At first he thought it was a lighter before noticing that it was a USB stick – an ordinary dark red USB stick. He picked it up, turned it over in his hand not knowing what to do with it and then slipped it into his jacket pocket.

His ensuing reading of the live skins was automatic, so preoccupied was his mind by the condensed memory lying deep in his pocket. That day, he barely heard Kowalski yelling, paid scant attention to Brunner's sardonic smiles. Even Yvon's lunchtime soliloquies failed to distract him from his thoughts. And that evening, the first thing he did on reaching home was not to feed Rouget de Lisle, as was his wont, but to rush over to his laptop and insert the memory stick, opening it up with a double click.

Guylain glowered at the nineteen-inch screen in frustration. The stick opened up a desert. Lost in the midst of the luminescent wilderness, the only folder it contained was prosaically called 'New folder' and did not promise anything very exciting. A gentle pressure of his index finger on the mouse unlocked the gates to the unknown. There were seventy-two text files called only by their respective numbers. Intrigued, Guylain moved the cursor to the first one and clicked apprehensively.

1.doc
Once a year, at the spring equinox, I do a recount.

Just to see, to make sure that nothing ever changes. At this very special time of year, when day and night share time equally, I do a recount with, lodged in the back of my mind, the ludicrous idea that perhaps, yes, perhaps one day, even something as unchanging as the number of tiles covering my dominion from floor to ceiling might change. It's as hopeless and stupid as believing in the existence of Prince Charming, but deep down inside me is that little girl who refuses to die and who, once a year, wants to believe in miracles. I know every one of my white tiles by heart. Despite the daily assaults with the sponge and detergent, many of them are still as shiny as on the first day and have preserved intact that slightly milky glaze covering the terracotta. To be honest, those aren't the ones I'm particularly interested in. There are so many of them that their perfection holds no charm. No, my attention is drawn rather to the injured, the cracked, the yellowing, the chipped, all those that time has maimed and which give the place, in addition to the slightly old-fashioned character that I've come to love, a touch of imperfection that I find strangely endearing. 'It is in the scars on the faces of the veterans that you can see wars, Julie, not in the photos of the generals in their starched, freshly pressed uniforms,' my aunt said to me once while we were the counting operation to note down the results in my spiral notebook. I push open the big swing door to the women's section with my shoulder.

There, I cast my sharp eyes over the mirror surround, the tiled surface around the washbasins, and the splashbacks. After inspecting each of the eight cubicles, gazing into the dark nooks and crannies to pick out the tiles hidden in the gloom, I do the same on the men's side, which is identical to the women's except for the six urinals gracing the back wall.

I sat down at the table, grabbed the electronic calculator from the drawer and impatiently entered the figures written down in my notebook. As always, my heart began to race as my finger pressed the EXE key for the grand total. And of course, as always, the same depressing number appeared on the screen: 14,717. I'm still dreaming of a warmer, rounder number, a more visually appealing number. A number containing a few nice bulbous zeros, even some deliciously plump eights, sixes or nines. A curvaceous three, as ample as a wet nurse's bosom, would be enough to make me happy. A number like 14,717, is all bones. It exposes its skinniness directly, assails your retina with its sharp angles. Whatever you do, once written down, it always remains a series of fractured straight lines. It would only take one tile more or less to give that unappealing number the beginnings of an attractive curve.

I put the calculator back in its case with a sigh. 14,717. Once again I'm going to have to be content with that ungainly number for the coming twelve months.

Guylain reread the piece three times, even though his eyes smarted with exhaustion from his day's labour. And each time, he felt the same enchantment in this woman's company. He made himself a strong black tea and printed all the documents out, then snuggled under the duvet to start on the second file. Late into the night, Guylain read each of the seventy-two entries, devouring them with pleasure. After skimming over the last page, he fell asleep, full of this Julie, and her little tiled world, who had just burst into his life.

16

That morning, Guylain counted nothing on his way to the station. Nothing. Not his footsteps or the plane trees, or the parked cars. For the first time, he didn't feel the need. In the dawn light, the graffiti tag on the metal shutter of *La Concorde* bookshop seemed more colourful than usual. He felt the pleasant weight of his leather briefcase in his right hand, swinging to the rhythm of his strides. Further down, he cleaved through the billows of hot fat spewing out non-stop from the small basement window of the butcher's shop, Meyer & Son, without the slightest feeling of nausea. Everything around him glistened and twinkled. The shower in the middle of the night had glazed each object, making it beautiful. At number 154, he did not fail to greet the old-man-in-slippers-and-pyjamas-under-his-raincoat. The old boy smiled with pleasure at the sight of Balthus, who was watering the base of his tree with a long, powerful stream.

Guylain climbed up the steps to the platform and stood on his white line. It stretched out into the greyness, whiter than ever. The 6.27 arrived on the dot of 6.27. The folding seat opened without protest when he lowered it. He took the cardboard folder out of the briefcase at his feet. Although the ritual was no different from any other day, it was plain to the more sharp-eyed observers that the young man's movements were less mechanical than usual. The disquiet that habitually set his features in a sad mask had vanished. Those same observers could also see that the blotting paper and onion skins had been replaced by ordinary A4 sheets. Without even waiting for the train to depart, Guylain began reading the first extract, labelled 8.doc, in a steady voice:

'I like to get to the shopping centre early. Slide my pass

into the electronic lock of the little side door at the far end of the car park. The unprepossessing steel door completely covered in graffiti is my entry point. As I walk down the central mall towards my domain, the only sound is that of my footsteps echoing off the shops' metal shutters. For the rest of my life, I will remember what my aunt said to me one day when she took me to work with her. All of eight years old, I scampered along beside her down this same mall. "You are the princess, my little Julie, the princess of the palace!" The princess has grown older, but the realm has barely changed. A completely deserted realm of over 100,000 square metres, awaiting only its subjects. I greet in passing the two beefy night security guards finishing their final walkabout before going home. They often say something nice about me. I always stop and stroke the head of their muzzled sheepdog as I go past. He's really a big softie, Nourredine, his master once told me. I love this particular moment when the planet seems to have stopped spinning, suspended between the nascent daylight and the darkness of the fading night. I tell myself that one day perhaps the earth will not resume its rotation and will stay frozen forever as night and day each stand firm in their respective positions, plunging us into a permanent dawn. Then I tell myself that, bathed in this crepuscular glow that gives everything a pastel hue, wars will perhaps be less ugly, famines less unbearable, peace more everlasting, the idea of having a lie-in less appealing and the evenings longer, and that only the white of my tiles will remain unchanged, preserving its lustre under the cold neon lights.

At the intersection of the three main malls, the big fountain sings its comforting glug glug. A few coins gleam at the bottom, coins thrown in by lovers or superstitious lottery players. I sometimes toss one in as I walk past, when I'm in the mood. Just for the pleasure of seeing it twinkle as it twirls down to the bottom. Perhaps too because that eight-year-old who's waiting for her Prince Charming to come and set her free at last is still inside me. A real Prince Charming who, having parked his magnificent steed in the car park (an Audi A3 or a DS with a leather interior, for instance), will pop into my dwelling to empty his bladder then sweep me up in his arms and carry me off for a protracted love affair. I'd better stop reading True Romance. *That stuff gets me all hormonal.*

I cascade down the fifteen stairs to my workplace in the bowels of the shopping centre. I insert my second fob to activate the mechanism that raises the metal shutter. It makes a terrifying clatter, as if, above my head, giant jaws are crunching the metal as it is swallowed up by the ceiling. Then I have an hour of "me time" until the doors open and the customers arrive. This is the hour I spend at my little camping table revising what I wrote the previous day and typing it onto my computer. I love the idea that my thoughts have matured overnight, like dough left to rise which you find in the morning all puffed-up and sweet-smelling. And to my ears, the clicking of the keys on my keyboard is the most beautiful music. When I've finished, I put my computer away in its case and don the sky-blue overall that is my uniform. A hideous polyester thing that makes me look like a post-office clerk from the 1970s. If people judge by appearances, then as my aunt would say, "Let Saint Harpic, the patron saint of lavatory attendants, be damned!"

It's time for Josy and breakfast. Josy (she hates being called Josiane) is the shampoo girl at the hair salon on the first floor. She is everything that I am not. She's in beauty; my world is ugly. She's frivolous; I'm more of the serious type. She's exuberant; I'm more uptight and repressed. Maybe that's why Josy and I get on so well. When she walks in, it's like a ray of sunshine. We tell each other our woes and our joys over a croissant and a coffee. We chat, we talk about our customers. How *this one asked for his hair to be dyed apple green, how another broke one of my flushes because the idiot hadn't realized you had to push not pull. We solve all the world's problems, tell each other our dreams and giggle like pubescent schoolgirls, then say have a nice day and see you tomorrow. Her day off is Tuesday. Tuesdays don't have the same flavour; there's an indefinable something missing, like a herb left out when cooking. I don't like Tuesdays.'*

Before leaving home, Guylain had substituted Julie's writings for the previous day's live skins. He did it without even asking himself why. It seemed completely natural to reconstitute little fragments of the young woman in the place where he had found them. He liked the idea that maybe one day, Julie herself would be sitting among them in that packed carriage listening to her own words.

'The 10 a.m. lard-arse came today. Always the same tactic. He charges down the stairs with his moronic hippopotamus tread and goes straight to his cubicle without even saying hello, nearly knocking over the table as he goes past. The 10 a.m. lard-arse never says hello or goodbye. Without a word, without a look, he

dives into the last cubicle, number 8. I've never seen him use any other cubicle. And if number 8 is occupied, then he waits, stamping his feet and kicking his heels outside the door, champing at the bit. This guy exudes smugness and uncouthness. The mug of an SUV driver who parks in the disabled parking bays. That guy's been coming once a week on the dot of ten to mess up number 8, making a racket that sounds like Armageddon, and I still haven't plucked up the courage to rebuke him even slightly even though he deserves it, he really does. Because when I say "mess up", it's not just a turn of phrase. Not to mention that this oaf uses up an entire roll of toilet paper each time and, of course, never takes the trouble to flush. I have to go in after his majesty's backside and spend nearly ten minutes making the place decent again. The worst thing is that this disgusting individual comes out of my cubicle number 8 as clean as a new pin, his jacket immaculate, the crease in his trousers in the right place, all hunkydory. But the drop of water that made the bidet overflow, as Aunty always says, is the tip. That adipose miser never leaves me more than one of those tiny five-cent coins, which he casually drops into my saucer. I always try to catch his eye, to signal my indignation, but that bastard has never dared look in my direction.

slouched against the Thing's control panel. Instead, Brunner came forward to meet him and followed on his heels, pursuing him into the changing room. The lanky fellow was jumping up and down and laughing nervously. Watching him circle round him like an excitable puppy, Guylain realized at once that he had something to tell him.

'What's up, Lucien?'

This was what Brunner had been waiting for. From his pocket he fished out a piece of paper with the company's letterhead and waved it under Guylain's nose with a broad grin:

'It's scheduled for May, Monsieur Vignolles. Five days in Bordeaux at the company's expense.' And the bastard had finally got his passport onto the next training course for a licence to operate the Zerstor. At last Brunner was going to fulfil his dream: starting up the wretched Thing. Guylain found it harder and harder to bear that psychopath's rapturous grins each time he sent a new bucket of books down into hell. It had always been his view that an executioner was duty-bound to remain impassive and not to show his feelings. Giuseppe had taught him to consider the multitude purely as a whole. 'Don't dwell on the details, kiddo. It will be easier, you'll see,' he had advised. If ill luck had it that a book managed somehow to catch Guylain's attention, then he would race to the Zerstor's arse end and gaze into the grey pulp until the image etched on his retina disappeared. Brunner did the opposite. That bastard derived a perverse pleasure from taking a close interest in what he was destroying. He would sometimes pull out a copy from the mountain and flick through it contemptuously before ripping off the cover and flinging the remains into the greedy maw. He knew that this upset Guylain and he often laid it on thickly. Then his voice would crackle in the headphones through the interference.

'Hey, Monsieur Vignolles, did you see, it's last year's Renaudot winner? They've still got their red wrap-around bands on!'

When he did this, even though it was strictly against the regulations, Guylain would kill the radio link so as not to have to put up with Brunner's despicable taunts. That morning, it took longer than usual for Guylain to lapse into the mindless state into which the Zerstor's incessant pounding inescapably plunged him. Julie was there with him, snuggled cosily under his hard hat. At lunch break, he wandered over to Yvon's hut and ate his way absently through a packet of savoury biscuits washed down with a cup of Yvon's black tea. His chewing was accompanied by Victor Hugo's *Ruy Blas*. Act III, Scene 2. Eyes closed, his head against the window that rattled at the sound of Yvon's powerful voice, Guylain listened as the verses of the slave in love with his queen filled the metal shack. Then he had the brainwave of introducing Yvon Grimbert to Magnolia Court. With a smile, Guylain pictured the security guard recounting the convoluted plots of these tragedies from another era to an audience of spellbound Magnolias. The man deserved a real audience, albeit an audience made up of ailing old folk. Guylain waited until Yvon had finished his speech before broaching the idea.

'Last Saturday, I went and gave a reading in a retirement home in Gagny. I'm going back this weekend. They're delightful people. They want me to come every Saturday. So I was thinking, Monsieur Grimbert, that it would be nice if you came with me and read something to them as well.'

Guylain had never managed to call Yvon by his first name. It was nothing to do with their age difference. He had no problem calling Giuseppe by his first name, even though he was older than the security guard. It was more a mark of esteem for his art. Yvon responded enthusiastically to the idea of exporting his voice beyond his tiny hut. Taken aback by his eagerness, Guylain, however, expressed some reservations as to the audience's ability to follow the rule of classical theatre's three unities. Yvon reassured him:

'Fie on wars of power, and on treasons sublime,
On all these dark princes, who will concoct their
* crime.*
History won't matter, as long as sings the rhyme
And a hope still lives on to reach the peak in time.'

As Yvon was already beginning to plan a programme of play readings going from Pierre Corneille to Molière and Jean Racine, Guylain reminded him that all this was still just a suggestion and that he would have to negotiate the arrangement with the Delacôte sisters. Guylain glanced at his watch and left hurriedly. He had an appointment at the occupational health clinic for his annual check-up at 1.30 sharp.

•

A pasty-looking healthcare assistant greeted him and asked him to remove all his clothes except his underpants. She weighed him, measured him, gave him a hearing test and an eye test, took his blood pressure and dipped a little stick in the bottle of urine he'd brought in. Five minutes later, a sun-bronzed doctor the colour of gingerbread called Guylain in for a summary check.

'Right, everything's fine, Monsieur . . . Vignolles . . . is that right, Guylain Vignolles? No particular problems to report? You appear to be in good shape, even though you are close to the lower limit of the curve.'

No, everything's not fine, Guylain felt like replying. *I'm waiting for the return of a father who died twenty-eight years ago. My mother thinks I'm an executive in a publishing company. Every night I tell a fish about my day. My job sickens me to the point that I sometimes puke my guts out. And to crown it all I'm falling under the spell of a girl I've never met. In a nutshell, then, no problems, except that in every single area of my life I am 'close to the lower limit of the curve', if you see what I mean.* Instead, Guylain gave a laconic 'I'm fine'. After a few recommendations on the importance of a healthy diet, the doctor scribbled his verdict at the bottom of the file. It was summed up in three words – three little words that entitled Guylain to continue the massacre with impunity: Fit for work.

That evening, Guylain went over to Giuseppe's. Sometimes he needed more than a goldfish to share his feelings. For nearly half an hour, he talked about the USB stick, explained how he had devoured the seventy-two documents it contained. He told Giuseppe excitedly about Julie; how the young woman wrote about her day-to-day life in little notebooks surrounded by 14,717 white tiles. The old man listened attentively and took in every word of what his friend was telling him.

'How can I find her? I don't know anything about her,' lamented Guylain. Giuseppe smiled.

'You know a lot more about her than you think. Don't be so defeatist,' Giuseppe reassured him. 'Do you think my legs grew back in a day?' he said, pointing to the shelves bowing under the weight of the Freyssinets. 'Have you got the stick with you? Download those files for me and I'll have a good look at them. There can't be that many toilets in shopping centres that have attendants.'

When Guylain left, Giuseppe pumped his hand profusely. 'I've got a feeling in my bones that you too will succeed in your quest,' murmured the old man with a smile.

18

Every Thursday evening, as the flashily dressed celebrity presenter with his smug, smart-arse face appeared on screen, Guylain telephoned his mother. Why Thursday and not another day, he couldn't say. That was just how it was, for no special reason. Over time, the Thursday evening phone call had become a ritual which he was duty-bound to honour. He knew she was there, comfortably ensconced in the living-room armchair, staring at the TV without really seeing it, locked in a permanent stupor since the departure of her husband that day in August 1984.

Twenty-eight years had now passed, but Guylain still couldn't say the word 'dead' when he spoke of his father. A child at the time, Guylain had visited his father for the last time a few days after the accident. He remembered an inert body lying in a hospital bed. For several long minutes, Guylain had been mesmerized by the tube entering his father's mouth. He had gazed in fascination at his face, which trembled with each movement of the infernal ventilator to the right of the bed. A man in a white coat had come to fetch his grandfather and had spoken of an imminent departure amid a stream of whisperings. So when two days later the little boy had seen on the TV those helmeted men in their impressive orange spacesuits waving to the crowds from the top of the gangway, his heart had leapt. Their lowered visors made it impossible to see their faces. They all had the same tube he had seen in the hospital coming out of their helmets. He was absolutely certain that his father was among those forms wading clumsily towards the hatch before vanishing inside the belly of the great spaceship. At 12.41 on 30 August 1984, before Guylain's eyes, the *Discovery* space shuttle took off from its launch pad with a deafening roar, carrying the six men up into space.

And when one hour later his grandmother came to tell him in an anguished voice that his father had departed, the only two words he could say in reply were 'I know'. All these years, the eight-year-old boy inside him had clung to the absurd hope that this father who was roving from star to star would come back one day. Nothing, not even the shovelfuls of earth thudding against the lacquered wood of the coffin, had managed to convince him otherwise.

His mother never answered before the third ring. Three rings, the time it took to rouse herself from her absence.

'Hello, Mum.'

'Oh! It's you.'

He smiled. Every week, she came out with the same reply as a prelude to the great game of questions and answers. What's the weather like in Paris? Had the latest transport strike caused him problems? Questions which he answered in the same evasive manner, already fearing the moment when he was going to have to lie to his own mother. The dreaded subject came up, as always: 'Still working in books?'

His mother knew nothing. Nothing of the pulping plant nor of his job of evil murderer. Years of deception, keeping quiet about the horror and inventing a better job, building an artificial life, just for her. The life of a Guylain who ate and drank things other than tasteless cereals and insipid tea; a Guylain who did not spend his days reducing tonnes of books to mush. This Guylain Vignolles did not share his life with a goldfish. Assistant publications manager at a print works, the Guylain he portrayed every Thursday evening, embraced life with open arms. The lie became more and more elaborate with each phone call, and each time he dreaded deep down that she would eventually get wind of his deceit when he faltered, despite the 400 kilometres between them. Guylain only went back to the village once or twice a year. Brief trips during which he spent most of his time escaping. Escaping his mother's questions; escaping unhappy memories and all the people who still called him Vilain Guignol, reviving the painful recollections it had taken him years to shake off; escaping a grave in which he had never believed.

And again this evening, as he put the receiver back after having pulled the wool over his mother's eyes once more, Guylain was unable to hold back any longer the rush of bile that assailed his throat.

19

The grey of the concrete has disappeared under the layer of slush covering the works floor. Ankles sunk in the foul-smelling sludge, he and Brunner are slinging heaped shovelfuls of muck into the Zerstor's funnel without a break. The Thing gobbles up all this mess, emitting a series of gross, squelchy slurps. Every ten seconds, its metal arse lays a new book which flies up towards the ceiling, its pages fluttering. Already, hundreds of books are swirling around the warehouse in an ominous swarm above the men's heads, making a deafening racket. From time to time, a book breaks away from the horde and plunges downwards, then corrects its path and whistles past their heads. A volume that is fatter than the others hits Brunner plumb on the side of his head. The great beanpole crumples into the sludge-filled trench. The poor man struggles frantically, but only becomes mired more deeply with each movement. The windows of Kowalski's office have been shattered into smithereens by the relentless assault of the flying book squadrons. Trapped in his tower, Fatso is unable to do anything. Despite the din, the terrible sound of books thumping against the boss's flabby flesh reaches Guylain's ears. Kowalski's howls echo through the works for nearly a minute before dying down for good. Guylain doesn't see it coming. A dictionary hurtling at full speed hits his right knee, knocking him over. A second breaks the handle of the shovel clean in two. He topples over head first, howling with pain. The sludge gushes into his gaping mouth, filling his lungs. He is choking. He gropes for something to hold on to until his fingers encounter a rope that appears out of nowhere.

The reading light fell and smashed at the foot of the bedside table, taking with it Rouget de Lisle's bowl, which shattered into a thousand pieces. The fish lay on the carpet amid the shards of glass, his fins quivering. His little body flashed orange with each spasm. Guylain grabbed the cereal bowl from the draining board and filled it with water, then threw in the dying Rouget. After one last spasm, the goldfish resumed his cruising speed as if nothing had happened and set off on a reconnaissance tour of the bowl, watched by a relieved Guylain.

Guylain winced. The nightmare had left him with a blinding headache and his forehead was throbbing. Not only was the Thing making his days a misery, it was increasingly sucking the lifeblood out of his nights. In the morning, he breakfasted on two effervescent tablets.

10.10. It was time for the second reading session at Magnolia Court. Same taxi, same route. And on his arrival, the warmest of welcomes. On spotting him, a flock of chirping grannies swooped down onto the steps and fluttered around him, their dentures chattering nineteen to the dozen. He almost forgot his headache. He shook hands right and left, tiny hands as rosy and delicate as pink champagne biscuits. They tapped his cheeks and smiled at him, devouring him with their eyes. He was the reader, the bearer of the good word. They called him Monsieur Vignal, Vignil, Vognal, Vagnul, Guillaume, Gustin, and simply Guy. Monique seemed to have infected the entire community during the week. He reserved his kisses for the two Delacôte sisters, who swooned with gratitude. The air reeked of eau de cologne, hair lacquer and traditional household soap. Sheltering in the huge lobby, the less robust residents slumped in their chairs, indifferent to the general excitement. People on their way out, forced to wait for a departure that was denied them.

Pushed by Josette, pulled by Monique, Guylain slipped between the two rows of living dead to enter the vast dining room, relieved to find it transformed into an auditorium. The podium was made of two tables on which the armchair had been placed. At this rate, thought Guylain, in a month he'd have his own dressing room, and in two, his statue in the grounds. The audience pushed and shoved and mumbled and grumbled, fighting over the best seats. Monique stepped in, ushering them to their places and getting them all to calm down. Asserting her authority, she allocated priority seats according to deafness and the various disabilities affecting the colony. *There are even more of them than last time,* mused Guylain. *Probably thanks to John and Gina and their shenanigans in the lorry.* He clambered up onto his throne, impatient to begin reading. With a discreet nod, Monique signalled that the session could begin. Josette confirmed with a stage wink.

'When you're a public lavatory attendant, wherever that may be, you're not expected to keep a diary and sit there tapping away on the keyboard of your laptop. You're only good for wiping from morning to evening, shining the chrome, scrubbing, polishing, rinsing, refurbishing the cubicles with toilet paper, and that's it. A loo attendant is meant to clean, not to write. It's OK for me to do crosswords, word searches, find-the-hidden-word, look for words locked up in all sorts of grids. It's also OK for me to read photostories, women's magazines or TV guides during my spare time, but for me to tap away with my fingers chapped by bleach on a laptop setting out my thoughts, that is beyond com-prehension. Worse, it arouses suspicion. It's as if there has been a misunderstanding, a miscasting. In the nether world, even a miserable twelve-inch laptop next to the tips saucer will always be a blot on the landscape.

I tried to use my computer at first, but I immediately saw from the sometimes outraged looks I received that this was most definitely not on. This "abnormal" behaviour met with a sort of refusal to understand, embarrassment and even rejection. I quickly had to come to terms with the fact that people generally expect only one thing of you: that you reflect back the image of what they want you to be. And they wanted none of this image that I was presenting. Mine was an attitude of the world above, an attitude that had no business down here. If I've learnt one thing in nearly twenty-eight years of life on this earth, it is that people judge by appearances, no matter what lies beneath the outer facade. So now, to allay suspicion, I pretend. The computer stays out of sight, neatly put away in its case at the base of my chair. People are more likely to leave a tip for a young woman sucking the end of her pen as she struggles to play spot-the-difference in the latest fashion magazine, than for the same young woman engrossed in the LCD screen of her state-of-the-art laptop. Fit docilely into the mould, slip into this lavatory attendant's costume – which is what I'm paid to do – and play the part, sticking closely to the script. It's easier for everyone, starting with myself. Besides, it reassures people. And as my aunt always says, auntologism number 11: A reassured customer will always be more generous than an anxious one. *I've got a notebook full of my aunt's auntologisms. I've been collecting them since I was ten years old and have built up a stock of them in a spiral-bound notebook which I always keep close at hand. I know them all by heart. Auntologism number 8:* Although a smile costs nothing, it can on the other hand earn you a lot. *Number 14:* Little errands don't bring in fat tips. *Number 5, the shortest, my favourite:* Peeing is no laughing matter.

Over time, I've learned to write while not appearing to do so. I fill my little notebooks on the rickety camping table that serves as my desk, scribbling amid the profusion of glossy magazines spread out in front of me. I advance in small steps. Not a single day goes by without my writing. Not to do so would be as if I hadn't lived that day, as if I had restricted myself to the role of loo-poo-puke cleaner that they want me to play, a poor creature whose only raison d'être *is the lowly occupation for which she is paid.'*

Guylain looked up. The audience seemed delighted. There was nothing oppressive about the silence that had come over the room. It was a light, digestive pause. On the faces scarred by the years, Guylain read something akin to wellbeing. He was delighted to share Julie's smooth white world with them.

'Where is it taking place?' asked a quavering voice, prompting a forest of arms to shoot up. Even before Monique had the time to channel the flow, the answers came thick and fast:

'In a swimming pool,' suggested one resident.

'At a spa,' proposed another.

'In a public lavatory,' mumbled a bald man in the front row.

'That doesn't make any sense, Maurice. We know it's in a lavatory, but there are public toilets everywhere. That doesn't tell us where it is.'

'A theatre,' piped up André enthusiastically. 'The old lady is a lavatory attendant in a theatre.'

'Why old, Dédé?'

'She's right, Maurice dear. Why old, can you tell us that, André?' spat the shrew who seemed to relish making poor old Dédé the butt of her spite.

'She's not old,' broke in a grandad in his Sunday best. 'It even says she's twenty-eight years old. And besides, she has a computer. She writes.'

'What is the world coming to if any old person

starts writing?' complained a grumpy soul sitting at the back of the room.

'Monsieur Martinet, you may have studied literature, but you don't have a monopoly on the subject,' scolded the retired primary-school teacher.

Monique asserted her natural authority and broke up the discussion. 'That's enough! Let's allow Guillaume to continue, please.'

Guylain stifled the laugh welling up inside him and moved on to the next excerpt:

'Thursday is a special day. It's the day my aunt comes. Sugar puff day. Sugar puffs are her drug. She needs her Thursday fix. Eight sugar puffs from her local bakery. Eight sugar puffs and nothing else. I've never seen her turn up with an éclair, a fruit tart or a vanilla slice. No, always eight little pastry puffs sprinkled with sugar crystals. Why eight and not seven or nine? That remains a mystery. Well, there's nothing particularly extraordinary about that, you'll say. True. But what does make it special is that my aunt doesn't go home to scoff her treats quietly in front of the TV, or to the nearest café to eat them out of the bag while sipping a hot chocolate or a lime-blossom tea. No, she hurries straight here, clutching her delicate treasure carefully

to her bosom. "You see," she explained once, "they don't taste the same anywhere else. I've tried, several times. I've even eaten some in the most beautiful places imaginable, the poshest tea rooms where dropped crumbs appear to turn into gold dust when they touch the floor, but it's only here that they release their full aroma and flavour. A real taste of heaven. It's as if the surroundings improve them. In here, my sugar puffs become extra special, whereas anywhere else, they're just good." I have to admit I was intrigued and wanted to try the experience for myself one time. Not with sugar puffs – they're not my thing – but with a waffle. I munch one from time to time, when I feel peckish. The crêperie on the ground floor makes excellent waffles. I always have a plain one and eat it at the counter, impatient to get back to my post. One day, I took my warm, crisp waffle and shut myself in one of the cubicles to eat it. Just to see. And I have to acknowledge that my aunt isn't entirely wrong. There was something different, as if my waffle was sublimated in the midst of all my tiles. I couldn't remember ever having eaten such a delicious waffle. When my aunt starts talking about her sugar puffs, she's unstoppable. "No comparison with those arrogant cakes that flaunt their cream, or all those pretentious biscuits covered in marzipan and collapsing under the weight of their own artifice," she blazes. "The sugar puff is to pastries what minimalism is to painting!" she announces to anyone who cares to listen. "Devoid of any illusionist effects, it presents itself to us in all its nakedness, its only adornment a few white crystals, offering itself up as it is: a little sweet with no other pretension than quite simply to be eaten." Oh, you should hear her – she's a real poet once she gets going.

"Have you reserved number 4 for me, darling?" she asks between kisses.

"Yes, Aunt. You know I always keep number 4 for you."

On Thursdays, I scrub cubicle 4 from top to bottom, then I lock it until she arrives. It's her perk. She has her cubicle here, the way others have their table at Fouquet's or their suite at the Hilton. She leaves her jacket, handbag and hat with me, then she toddles over, clutching her bag of sugar puffs, her cushion wedged under her arm, her eyes already shining greedily. For nearly twenty minutes, comfortably seated on the soft cushion placed on top of the seat cover, she wolfs down her treasures one by one, crushing the pastry against the roof of her mouth with her tongue to release the vanilla flavoured aroma *locked up inside the pastries onto her taste buds. "Julie, if only you knew!" she exclaims when she comes out. "God, it's good!" A real junkie who's just had eight fixes one after the other.'*

The clock over the dining-room door already showed 11.25. The taxi would be there any minute. The audience did not seem in a hurry to resume their day-to-day life. Conversations were in full swing. The ladies recalled their recipes for choux pastry, each of them sharing her little secrets. The number of eggs, the amount of butter, the right piping-nozzle to use. Some of them were holding forth about the wisdom of eating sugar puffs with one's buttocks glued to a toilet seat. While some found the notion absolutely ridiculous, others were not against the idea of smuggling their dessert from the lunch table into their room for a tasting session seated on their toilet.

Guylain tore himself from the comfy armchair. He felt better and better among his Magnolias. Monique and Josette each offered him an arm to help him back onto terra firma. He took advantage of the lull to raise the subject of Yvon. The two sisters said they would be delighted to welcome an additional reader to their residence and agreed, providing the session could be extended by half an hour. Guylain saw no reason why not. He kissed them, inhaling a parting whiff of eau de cologne before going out to the taxi that had just come into view at the end of the drive.

20

Rouget de Lisle V had died during Guylain's absence. He found the fish's little body lying next to the bowl when he came home from Magnolia Court. His replacement aquarium must have felt too narrow for him to be able to stretch his fins properly and Rouget had preferred to take the great leap into the unknown, to find out whether the world wasn't better elsewhere. *His final dream of freedom was shattered on the cold stainless steel of my draining board*, thought Guylain ruefully. He delicately picked up the tiny corpse, holding the tail between his thumb and forefinger, and slipped it into a plastic bag. In the early afternoon, he went out, heading in the direction of Les Pavillons-sous-Bois.

Guylain knew the way by heart, having made the trip four times before. After a twenty-minute walk, he stopped halfway across the bridge over the Ourcq canal, extracted Rouget de Lisle's already stiff body and threw it into the calm waters. 'Peace upon your little fish bones, my brother.'

He had never been able to dispose of his deceased fish by throwing them into the rubbish chute like ordinary waste. To him they were a bit more than mere ornamental fish. Each one took with it Guylain's most intimate secrets locked in its gills. In the absence of a mighty river, the Ourcq canal was the noblest grave he had been able to find. After a parting glance at the orange streak descending into the murky depths, Guylain retraced his path with a brisk step. A quarter of an hour later, the bell above the door of the pet shop tinkled cheerily as he stepped inside. His entrance was greeted by a chorus of squawking budgies, yapping puppies, mewing kittens, squealing rabbits and cheeping chicks. Only the fish were silent, content to send up the occasional stream of bubbles.

'Can I help you?' The assistant was just like her surly voice. Cold and pale.

'I need a goldfish,' mumbled Guylain. Need – that was indeed the word. He was truly addicted to the golden creatures. Guylain could no longer cope without that silent, colourful presence gracing his bedside table. From experience, he knew that there was a vast difference between living alone and living alone with a goldfish.

'What type?' asked the anaemic girl, opening a fat catalogue. 'We have Lionheads, Comets with long forked tails, red-capped Orandas, Pompoms, Ryukin, Shubunkin, Ranchu or Black Moors – very original with their dark colouring. Our top-selling variety right now is the Celestial Eye with its double tail and telescope eyes turned upwards. Very trendy.'

Guylain wanted to ask if they didn't have the standard model, the ordinary goldfish with two little eyes on either side of its head, where they should be. For what it did – swim round and round – that was perfectly sufficient. Instead, he pulled out of his pocket the tattered photo of Rouget I, the father of the dynasty, the one who had started it all, and waved it under the assistant's nose: 'I would simply like the same as this one,' he said, tapping the tired image.

The girl inspected the photo with an experienced eye and led him to the big aquarium at the back of the shop where around fifty potential Rouget de Lisles were swimming around. 'I'll leave you to make up your mind. Just call me when you're ready. I'll be next door,' she said, holding out a net.

She had no interest in him and his common-or-garden goldfish. Photo in hand, Guylain gazed at the orange display swirling in front of him in search of the perfect clone. He soon spotted one. Same colour, slightly paler on the sides, same fins, same affable eyes. After three fruitless attempts to net it, he caught it on the fourth. He inquired about a new bowl too.

'Spherical or rectangular?' asked the assistant. Cruel dilemma to have to choose between a deadly monotonous circular path or a halting circuit that's all sharp angles. In the end he opted for the usual glass globe. Even for the most common of fish, there could be no worse ordeal than constantly banging into corners.

Back home, Guylain hurriedly poured in a bed of white sand, laid the previous tenant's miniature amphora on it and planted the synthetic seaweed. Soon, a new Rouget de Lisle was happily splashing around in this fairy-tale decor. This tiny fish, which was the spitting image of its brothers, exuded a sense of immortality that Guylain found pleasing. For a fleeting second he thought he saw in Rouget VI's eye the full acknowledgement of his five predecessors.

was convinced that the mutt had probably reached the end of the road and that it wouldn't be long before he joined Rouget V in the great animal kingdom in the sky. It was a well-known fact, old dogs nearly always began to die from the rear. Guylain took his leave of the old fellow with a parting bow of the head that was more like an expression of condolence, and continued on to the station. He felt a genuine pleasure as he sat down on his folding seat. Julie was burning his fingers.

'Saturday is always the busiest day of the week, along with Wednesday, but when Saturday is also the last day of the sales, then you can tell a mile off that it's going to be a horrendous day, the kind of day when even the shopping centre's 100,000 square metres seem to be hard put to hold so many people. It was packed from the minute the doors opened. Hordes of visitors poured into my cave all day long to deposit their stream of urine, excrement, blood and even vomit. Sometimes I see them reduced purely to sphincters, stomachs, intestines and bladders on legs and no longer as entire human beings. I don't particularly like these peak shopping days which turn the shopping centre into a giant ant hill. I find all this frantic activity disturbing,

even though it often heralds excellent takings. You have to be on your toes the whole time so as to keep up. Restock the cubicles with toilet paper; don't forget to wipe the seats as soon as you get a chance; chuck bleach blocks into the urinals regularly, not forgetting to sit by the saucer as often as possible. Thank you, goodbye. Thank you, have a nice day. Hello, thank you, good-bye. The thing is that a lot of them don't give anything if there's no witness to appreciate their generosity. Auntologism number 4: Beggar absent, begging bowl empty. *I think the entire human race has come by here today. That's what I said to myself as I locked the gates, exhausted, my back broken, my nostrils saturated with the smell of bleach and ammonia.*

I far prefer the midweek early-morning calm with its slow trickle of customers to these fraught periods. When it's like this, I sometimes put aside my writing or my magazines to listen to them. Holding my breath, my eyes closed, I ignore the constant rumble of the shopping centre and concentrate all my attention on the noises coming from the toilets. My hearing has become more refined over time and now I'm able to identify each of the sounds that reach me through the closed doors, no matter how muffled, without hesitation. My aunt, armed with her characteristic bleach-infused omniscience, classified these noises into three main categories. First of all there are the ones she prettily calls "noble sounds". The discreet click of a belt being unbuckled, the gentle whoosh of a zip being pulled down, the snap of a press stud, as well as all those rustlings of fabrics – silks, nylon, cottons and other materials that sing against the skin with a rippling, crinkling, swishing, and other murmurings. Then come what she calls the "cover-up sounds". Embarrassed coughing, deceptively cheerful whistling, activating the flush – all those sounds designed to drown out the third category, that of "active sounds": flatulence, gargling, tinkling, the song of the enamel, the plopping of high dives, the toilet roll unspooling, the paper tearing. And I would add a final category, rarer but O so interesting – sounds of relief, all those grunts and groans and sighs of contentment that sometimes rise up to the ceiling when the floodgates open and that liberating stream held in for too long cascades onto the enamel, or the sonorous avalanche of over-full bowels. Sometimes I love people when they fetch up here, so vulnerable in their need to relieve their bladder or empty their stomach. And during the brief time that they are hidden from view behind the cubicle doors, whatever their condition or social status, I know they are returning to the dawn of time, mammals satisfying the call of nature, their buttocks glued to the seat, their trousers corkscrewed around their calves, their forehead dripping with sweat as they labour to open their sphincter, alone with themselves, far from the world above. But the people here do not only leave me the contents of their bowels or their bladder. It's not unusual for some of them to relieve themselves in here and then come over to me to pour out their woes. I listen to people. I let them vent their gall, wring out their little lives, chat to me about their various prob-lems. They confide, they moan, they cry; they're jealous, they tell their stories. Auntologism number 12: Toilets are confessionals without a priest. *Luckily there are others who come and chit-chat for the simple pleasure of exchanging a few pleasantries, and for whom I am more than just two ears there to listen to their sorrows. I've put a visitors' book at the exit, like in some famous restaurants – a visitors' book where people can leave me, in addition to a small coin, a memento of their visit in the form of a message. And every night, when I close up, I draw in my nets and take a few moments to skim through these words of love or loathing,* ranging from the sublime to the ridiculous, which will always teach me a lot more about human nature than any encyclopaedia.

"Beautifully clean. Isabelle"

"Better than a mere public toilet. A clean, very well-maintained haven. Keep it up. René"

"You should have stayed on at school, stupid cow! X"

"Your paper is a bit rough for my taste, otherwise everything was perfect. Marcelle"

"We were just passing through, but we'll be back for the simple reason that your toilets are immaculately clean. Xavier, Martine and their children, Thomas and Quentin"

"Suck my dick, bitch."

"Kings and philosophers defecate, and so do ladies. Montaigne"

"It would be good to have magazines available in the cubicles. Furthermore, it is somewhat annoying that there is no choice of soap. It would be nice to be able to choose one's own fragrance. The place is clean (other than a few stains around the washers – try white vinegar). Madeleine de Borneuil"

"I had a wank in your crappy toilet thinking about you, you slag."'

There were a few laughs in the compartment mingled with exclamations of indignation. Guylain looked up. Most of the commuters were looking at him encouragingly. He half smiled and then launched into another of Julie's diary entries:

'I wouldn't swear to it, but it looks to me as though it's got even bigger. Not a lot, only a few centimetres, but at this rate, it could reach the big mirrors on the women's side before the end of the decade. My aunt told me that the crack appeared nearly thirty years ago, when they demolished the central staircase to put in the new escalators. It was born under the first batter-ing of the pneumatic drill, pointing its nose towards the north corner, under the basins, and then it began to spread. It wasn't very wide at the time, barely a hair's breadth and not much longer than a blade of grass, but it has grown wider as it has crept over the white expanse, streaking each of the tiles it met on the way with a thin, dark line. Its advance has never halted; it continues on its way without ever deviating an inch from its path, no matter what obstacles it

encounters. It was born under Mitterrand, celebrated its first metre before the Russians left Afghanistan and its second metre as Pope John-Paul was being buried. Now it is over three metres long. It's like a wrinkle on a face, marking the passage of time. I'm fond of this fissure that somehow continues its path, tracing its own destiny without giving the slightest consideration to the planet's ups and downs.'

When the train pulled into the station and the passengers alighted, an outside observer would have had no trouble noticing how Guylain's listeners stood out from the rest of the commuters. Their faces did not wear that off-putting mask of indifference. They all had the contented look of an infant that has drunk its fill of milk.

22

It was 7 p.m. when Guylain rang Giuseppe's bell. Exceptionally, the old boy had contacted him at work in the middle of the afternoon. He had phoned Kowalski and asked to speak to Guylain. Suddenly Felix Kowalski's voice, sounding even angrier than usual, reached Guylain's ears through his radio head-phones. Kowalski didn't like his staff being disturbed when they were hard at work.

'Vignolles, telephone.'

Guylain snatched the receiver from Fatso's out-stretched hand, wondering who on earth could be calling him at the plant.

'Can you come by after work?'

'Yes, why?'

Giuseppe's only reply was a brusque, 'You'll find out,' before hanging up. And again that evening, Giuseppe kept Guylain on tenterhooks while they had an aperitif, even though it was obvious that the old boy was bursting to tell him something. He kept rolling his wheelchair backwards and forwards, clumsily grabbing little handfuls of pistachios and peanuts, constantly squirming in his chair. Unable to contain himself any longer, Guylain finally came out with the question he had been burning to ask since his arrival: 'You haven't brought me here simply to drink a glass of Moscato, have you, Giuseppe?'

'I haven't been sitting here twiddling my thumbs in your absence, you know, kiddo.' There was a mischievous glint in his eye. He executed a half-turn and invited Guylain to follow the wheelchair into the bedroom, which doubled as his office. The room was in a glorious state of disarray. The rickety desk was buried under piles of documents. The computer and printer had been relegated to the floor to make room. The hospital bed itself had not been spared by the tidal wave and it too was covered in loose sheets of paper. There was a huge map of Paris and the surrounding region with scrawled notes all over it tacked to the wall at wheelchair height. Several circles had been crudely drawn in red felt-tip. In other places, identical rings had been crossed out. Some names of towns were underlined, others deleted. Post-its covered in the illegible, spidery handwriting understandable only to Giuseppe blossomed everywhere in the capital and its suburbs. The map was a mass of deletions, alterations and stuck-on notes. The room resembled a wartime military HQ.

'What the hell's this mess, Giuseppe?'

'Oh, that! You can't say it happened all by itself. Two whole days to draw up an inventory and another two days to sort and refine the data. It wasn't easy, but I'm pretty chuffed. I finished this morning.'

'Finished what, Giuseppe?'

'Your Julie, of course. Do you or don't you want to find her? I read the whole thing three times, you know, to be sure not to overlook any clues. Rather thin on the ground, they are. She's pretty stingy on the detail, your young lady. In the seventy-two files, she doesn't once mention her surname or even the name of the town where she works. A really accomplished author. But it takes more than that to deter old Giuseppe.'

'I started with this,' he went on, placing a piece of paper in Guylain's hands. 'We know her name is Julie, that she's a lavatory attendant, that she's twenty-eight and that once a year, at the spring equinox, the young lady counts her tiles, which number 14,717. But I particularly noted clues 4, 9 and 11, the most important ones: her toilets are in a shopping centre. This centre has an area of 100,000 square metres and is at least thirty years old, as evidenced by the crack.'

Guylain stared in disbelief at the brief list in front of his eyes. Clues 4, 9 and 11 had been highlighted in green. Giuseppe then explained the methodology he had used to create the huge rainbow-coloured hodgepodge tacked to the wall. He had googled all the major shopping centres in Paris and the sur-rounding region and come up with a list of eighteen centres, mainly in the inner suburbs. Then he had gone over the details of each one with a fine-tooth comb to find out when they were built, so as to elim-inate the most recent. That way he had ruled out Le Millénaire in Aubervilliers, Val d'Europe in Marne-la-Vallée and Carré Sénart in Lieusaint, all three too recent. A second sifting process based on surface area had whittled his list down to eight finalists. And Giuseppe proudly declaimed the names of the lucky winners, pointing to them on the map with a ruler, detailing their pedigrees:

'O'Parinor in Aulnay, 1974, 90,000 square metres. I know, it's not 100,000 but I kept it in anyway. Rosny 2, 1973, 106,000 square metres. Créteil Soleil, 1974, 124,000 square metres. Belle Épine in Thiais, 1971, 140,000 square metres. A bit big, but anyway. Évry 2, 1975, bang on 100,000 square metres. Vélizy 2, built in 1972, 98,000 square metres. Parly 2, in Le Chesnay, 1969, 90,000 square metres. Like Aulnay, just under, but why not? And the last one, Les Quatre Temps in La Défense, 1981, 110,000 square metres. They all have a public toilet but I wasn't able to check whether there's an attendant. It doesn't say that anywhere on the website – anyone would think it's taboo.'

Guylain was impressed with his old friend's efficiency. He examined the little red dots which, if you joined them together, formed a magnificent ellipse from Aulnay in the north-east to Nanterre in the west, skirting south round the capital. Only Évry sat outside this imaginary curve and remained isolated at the bottom of the map. When Guylain ventured to suggest that Julie might well work in a centre in the provinces, Giuseppe was incensed.

'Your memory stick, it wasn't on the Paris–Bordeaux or the Paris–Lyon intercity train that you found it; it was on the commuter train, so it looks to me as if there's a strong chance that your Julie isn't cleaning loos anywhere but near Paris! And if I were you, I'd start looking in O'Parinor and Rosny 2 – they're the closest.'

They spent the rest of the evening in front of an Italian TV dinner concocted by Giuseppe. On leaving his friend, Guylain promised he'd keep him up to date with his progress. He went home with the precious list tucked carefully away in his jacket pocket. And while Rouget VI wolfed down the flakes floating on the surface of his bowl, Guylain read to him the names of the eight centres upon which all his hopes were pinned: the eight stations of the cross.

23

Guylain spent the first half of the week checking out the shopping centres. As soon as he clocked off, he rushed away from the Zerstor, tore off his overalls and left the works without even showering, and ran for the train, bus or first suburban connection that came along, depending on that day's target. Monday, O'Parinor at Aulnay. Tuesday, Rosny 2. Wednesday, Créteil Soleil. And the previous evening, La Défense – all mirages that vanished one by one. Each night, curious and impatient, Giuseppe inquired about Guylain's progress.

'Well?'

'Well nothing.' And each time he would explain wearily that yes, there were toilets, yes, there was a lavatory attendant but no one who even remotely resembled a nondescript twenty-eight-year-old woman. At Aulnay, he came across a sour-tempered old bag, at Rosny, a skinny guy with a moustache, at La Défense, a cheerful woman from the Ivory Coast wearing a multicoloured boubou, and finally, a girl with a shaven head covered in piercings. Giuseppe was even more crestfallen than he was.

'It's not possible,' he mumbled to himself, 'that's the only place she can be.' Guylain would reply that tomorrow was another day, then hang up and slump on his bed.

That morning, the old-man-in-slippers-and-pyjamas-under-his-raincoat greeted Guylain effusively. Balthus was back. A Balthus who was wearing himself out trying to water the roots of his favourite plane tree. 'You were right,' said his elated master, tapping Guylain on the shoulder as he drew level. 'My Balthus is back to his old self. Just look at him.' Guylain nodded, glancing warily at the mutt whose hindquarters were sagging and still trailing a little.

That's what death is like, he thought. The bitch was sometimes content to send out little barbs and then return to other occupations. But he was certain that it wouldn't be long before she came back to finish off the job. In the meantime, Guylain reckoned that Balthus's return augured well for the day. Once again, reading extracts from Julie's diary on the train restored his optimism.

'I shouldn't boast about it but I did it, I screwed over the 10 a.m. lard-arse. And when I say screwed, I mean well and truly. It was easy. I roped in my friend Josy, who agreed to be my accomplice at once. I didn't ask much of Josy, just to give me fifteen minutes of her time. I know that my favourite shampoo girl would have given me a whole day of her holiday to knock that oaf off his pedestal. It was auntologism number 3 that inspired me: In the toilets, power belongs to the person who has the paper.*

Technically, the trap was easy to set. I opened up the paper dispenser, removed the roll that was inside, sellotaped a single sheet to the edge and closed the lid, taking care to allow the sheet of toilet paper to poke through the slit – the reassuring evidence that there was a roll of paper inside. The classic schoolboy prank.

Practically – and that's where Josy came in – I had to make sure that the 10 a.m. lard-arse got caught in the trap and not an innocent passing customer. So all Josy had to do was occupy the gentleman's favourite cubicle and wait, mobile phone in hand, for me to text her alerting her to the bastard's arrival. On the dot of ten, his heavy footsteps echoed on the stairs. Light beige suit, green tie and a brown shirt. I beeped Josiane, who came out with her head down, having taken care to flush so as not to arouse suspicion. I don't think old fatty even realized that a woman had just come out of the men's toilets, so preoccupied was he with preparing to deposit his disgusting morning catch. Josy stuck around to watch what happened next. I'll spare you the details, but judging from the noises we heard coming from number 8, it sounded as though he was letting rip as never before. The silence that followed was all the more hilarious. I thought I even heard a slight crackling of the toilet paper as it came away from the sellotape holding it in place. Less than two minutes later, the 10 a.m. lard-arse came out, his face purple, his shirt half tucked into his trousers, his jacket more crumpled than a two-week-old lettuce. He crossed my realm with the slow gait of a penguin crossing an ice floe. And for the first time, I caught the look on his face. It was the look of someone in shock, someone who had just seen pride spattered with his own shit. As he walked past, I jerked my head at the saucer and indulged in a 'Service, thank you'. The 10 a.m. lard-arse didn't put anything in it. Besides, he wasn't in a state to put anything anywhere. But the sight Josy and I were treated to as he attempted to go up my stairs with his shit-covered buttocks clenched will forever be one of the best tips I've ever received.'

Surprised at first, Guylain greeted the applause that broke out in the compartment with a smile. The young woman's revenge had delighted the audience. He had to force himself to put the picture of a Kowalski, scarlet with shame, out of his mind, so as to concentrate on the next excerpt:

'Speed dating. The phrase itself sounds inoffensive, but it scares me. Josy knows it does, but she'd been on and on at me for days over our morning coffee and croissants before I finally agreed to sign up with her for this "date with love", as she calls it. For discerning singles only, for an entrance fee of twenty euros with one complimentary drink, said the flyer. I don't know why I said I would. Maybe Josy's unshakeable

enthusiasm. Or that little girl deep inside me who's still waiting for her Prince Charming and makes me toss a coin in the fountain from time to time.

"What's the worst thing that can happen?" she said.

"Meeting an arsehole who's only come to get laid, who treats the whole thing like a cattle market?"

"So? You're smart enough to clock him and tell him to go and have a wank like a poor lonesome cowboy."

Josy's always very forthright. What bothers me about the expression "speed dating" is mainly the word speed. It sounds like a quickie. I don't like that wham-bam-thank-you-ma'am attitude. Of course, Josy and I were immediately accepted, given our backgrounds. Single, young, not too bad-looking based on current beauty criteria which favour curves over the emaciated forms of the anorexic models who have graced the fashion pages for years. On the job front, I had to cheat a bit, of course. I wasn't going to write "Profession: lavatory attendant". That would attract every weirdo on the planet and put off all the others. Lab assistant. Again, that was Josy's idea.

"A lab assistant cleans tiles from dawn till dusk too," she assured me. "It's just that in your case, it's loos and in hers it's tiled work surfaces, but at the end of the day it boils down to the same thing."

Seven dates, each lasting seven minutes – that's what you get with speed dating. There are rules. You mustn't exchange personal contact details, for example (no chance of me doing that anyway). After each seven-minute date, you have to give a confidential appraisal of your date and say whether you want to see them again or not.

Josy waited for me at the shopping centre exit. The ceremony – I don't know what else to call it – was due to start at 8.30 p.m. That didn't leave me the time to go home, so I got changed at work. I had to redo my make-up several times. First I put on too much eye-shadow and not enough lipstick. Then I overdid the gloss, but didn't apply enough mascara. Each time, I contemplated the painted tart in the mirror gazing back at me with annoyance. Result, I ended up wiping it all off with lashings of make-up remover and made do with a spritz of Lolita Lempicka in the hollow of my throat. Clothes-wise I'd decided that my Lee Coopers, ballerina pumps and the little white heather-effect blouse bought at the sales would do fine. For the finishing touch, a silk scarf knotted casually round my neck was supposed to make me look relaxed, which I wasn't at all – far from it. The last time I felt so nervous was at my oral exams for the baccalaureate.

Josy, on the other hand, had pulled out all the stops. Figure-hugging dress, hair extensions, heels and Chanel N° 5. A sexy, modern Cinderella. At the door, they checked our IDs and gave us a voucher for a free drink. Josy and I wished each other good luck.

"It's going to work," she said, crossing her fingers.

To be honest, all I wanted to do was take to my heels, go home and snuggle under the duvet with a good book. Instead, I did as all the other girls did: I sat down at the first free table I could find and ordered a mint cordial. The first guy who came and sat opposite me told me he was a teacher of something or other. He did nothing but talk about himself, without asking me a single question. When the bell rang seven minutes later, I hadn't even been able to get a word in. The only two words I'd uttered were hello and goodbye. For seven minutes I'd been sitting opposite a navel. A second guy sat down in the still-warm seat. Then a third. And every seven minutes, the bell rang throughout the bar, like a guillotine coming down. Next. It reminded me of a polite, friendly merry-go-round. Hello ma'am, goodbye ma'am, thank you ma'am. A sort of country dance where you have to change partners each time the moron holding the broom handle thumps the floor with it. Despite meeting seven men,

I confess I was left feeling hungry, even though I hadn't come here particularly famished. None of them seemed attractive enough for me to aspire to being carried off on his white steed. When they were OK physically, there was something wrong mentally, and vice versa. Some of them were very nice, like the cultured, interesting young man who had travelled widely but who had a gross, hairy wart on his chin which overshadowed all the rest. During the seven minutes, that's all I saw, that bulbous growth covered in hideous, thick black hairs. On the form I just wrote "off-putting wart", before going on to the next. There was this other guy – the third, I think – not bad-looking, very tall, but whose lisp gave his conversation a pathetically funny twist, a conversation in which each "s" was torture for the poor guy. The high point was when he told me his job. I simply couldn't stop the giggles that I'd managed to stifle from erupting, which put an early end to our date. Staring down into my mint cordial, I took advantage of the two minutes' respite before the jingling bell to pull myself together. But shit, when you've got a lisp, you don't want to be a "thothial thientitht"! My fifth was called Adrien and he was so uptight that I was convinced he must be autistic. Unlike the first, who hadn't let me get a word in edgeways, this one sat there silent as the tomb for the four hundred and twenty seconds of our date. Four hundred and twenty seconds during which he writhed on his chair and kneaded his hands as if trying to stop them flying away. When I asked him a question, he turned as red as if he were constipated and straining to have a shit. Constipated types have always made me feel uneasy. And in my job, there's no shortage. As Aunty always says, "You can expect anything from a constipated person, even nothing. A constipated person is to the toilet as a mute is to singing, and vice versa." The fourth and sixth were from the same mould. Middle-class, straight-A types and the manners of upwardly mobile executives, the sort who change their shirt and shave twice a day. As for the last one, he had a dick for a brain. His only concern seemed to be to find out whether I was vaginal or clitoral. I told him that my star sign was Pisces with ascendant Aquarius, but sex-wise I wasn't yet sure where I stood. And I made it clear to that jerk that the day I made up my mind, I certainly wouldn't be calling on him to check where my orgasm was going to come from. In the end, I found myself with an empty glass and seven appraisals that read like a chamber of horrors. 1: Navel of the world; 2: Off-putting wart; 3: Lisp; 4: Suit; 5: Chronic con-

stipation; 6: *Another suit*; 7: *Sex maniac. I had to go home by taxi because Josy was nowhere near done. After this first round, she had five requests. Five out of seven. Whereas two of my dates wanted to meet me again, the wart and suit number two. I left without replying. The latest Stephen King was waiting by my bed.*'

Guylain remembered with amusement the first time he had skimmed through document number 70. The ten-minute read had been agonizing. A round of Russian roulette, tortured by the possibility that the Prince Charming Julie dreamed of might appear at any moment and steal her heart away. He had reached the end of that entry with a sigh of relief.

24

His head on the pillow, Guylain lay watching
Rouget swimming round and round in his bowl.
What dream could he be pursuing that kept him
going without ever giving up? Perhaps he was
chasing himself without realizing it, his head in
the slipstream created by his own movement?
During the past few days, Guylain had been afraid
that he too was pursuing nothing but an illusion.
The previous evening, his visit to Belle Épine in
Thiais had been unsuccessful. A week of fruitless
searching, chasing a phantom. He only believed
that Julie was real because of her writing, just as

Rouget believed there was an intruder in his bowl from swimming in its wake all day long.

Guylain had arranged to meet Yvon at the taxi rank at the top of the avenue. As usual, the security guard wore a beautifully tailored suit and proudly sported a white carnation in his buttonhole. The two men clambered into the taxi booked ten minutes earlier.

> *'Drive on, my good coachman, avoiding jolts*
> *and bends.*
> *With your expert handling take us to journey's*
> *end.*
> *Be lively and alert. Advance, for pity's sake,*
> *And lead this carriage forth, our gold is here*
> *at stake.'*

The driver shot them an anxious look in his rear mirror before setting off. It took three red lights before the frown on his forehead disappeared completely.

With his immaculate pencil moustache, the majestic way he held his head and his impeccable dress, Yvon immediately made a strong impression on the fair sex at Magnolia Court. Even Josette, after rapidly depositing her excess lipstick on Guylain's cheeks, was unable to resist the desire to join the cluster that had formed around the newcomer. When Yvon spoke, between hand-kissings, his resonant bass voice charmed even the most impervious of the ladies:

'*Ne'er did such a manor in these lands far away*
Do me the great honour of having me to stay.'

'Oh! Monsieur Grinder, you flatter us,' breathed Josette Delacôte, choked with joy.

Welcome to the club of maimed surnames, thought Guylain. As tall Yvon strode regally towards the hall, surrounded by this court already won over to his cause, Guylain followed the procession, smiling, relegated to the role of footman that now seemed to be his. Yvon's voice boomed through the hall, sending a thrill through the two rows of slumped bodies on either side of the door:

'*Lord, how great this hall is, so stately and so fine,*
No entry is so close to the heavens sublime.
Happy are the tenants that may enjoy the chance
To have so fine a place to finish their last dance.'

Guylain feared for a moment that this noisy intrusion into the perpetual fog that filled the heads of the residents might cause a stroke or a heart attack. Even if no one contradicted Yvon, Guylain wasn't convinced that all those poor drooling wretches in their incontinence pads were in a state to appreciate how lucky they were to finish their dance in such beautiful surroundings. After a tour of the upstairs, where some of the bolder residents insisted on showing the new visitor their rooms, Yvon commentated his visit in two succinct lines:

'The apartments I've found are much like the
tenants:
In some, distress abounds, others are quite
pleasant.'

Although the rhyme scheme sometimes required a certain poetic licence that did not always reflect reality, Guylain had to admit that his assessment of the place and its occupants was spot on. Monique gave herself the honour of introducing Yvon to the audience, de-baptising him once by calling him Yvan Gerber and then Johan Gruber, before dubbing him Vernon Pinder, which was the name she finally adopted. Poor Yvon was no longer quite so high and mighty seeing his name mangled by the Delacôte sister. Guylain mounted the podium to read an excerpt from Julie. From the outset, it was apparent that he didn't have the audience's attention. Even though they sat silently amid the usual coughs, scraping of chairs and tapping of sticks, they were still unruly in anticipation of Yvon's performance. Guylain decided to curtail his reading. End of the first half, and now the headline act. The king of the alexandrine pushed away the armchair that Guylain offered him with a theatrical gesture, reminding him of one of the fundamental rules for reciting poetry:

'*No matter who's speaking, it is no mystery*
One must be upstanding so the air can flow free.'

So with no script and no other safety net than his phenomenal memory, Yvon Grimbert, alias Vernon Pinder, subjected the ears of the astounded audience to a first blast. Phaedra's speech declaring her love for Hippolytus, Act II, Scene 5:

'Ah, yes for Theseus
I languish and I long, not as the Shades
Have seen him, of a thousand different forms
The fickle lover, and of Pluto's bride
The would-be ravisher, but faithful, proud
E'en to a slight disdain, with youthful charms . . .'

One speech ran into the next, as Yvon switched with virtuosity from a ranting Don Diego to an anguished Andromaque, then an impassioned Britannicus to a patriotic Iphigenia. Without taking her eyes off Yvon for a second, Monique asked Guylain what Yvon's profession was.

'Alexandrophile,' he replied without batting an eyelid.

'Alexandrophile,' repeated the old lady softly, her eyes shining with admiration.

Guylain made himself scarce before the end of the session, leaving his friend in the care of the Delacôte sisters who had invited Yvon to have lunch with them. By way of acceptance, the thespian came out with a verse of his own composition:

'Never would I dream that this fortune could be
*   mine*
To share in such feasting in company so fine.'

Less than ten minutes later, Guylain emerged from the taxi and dived into the station. Évry 2, its 100,000 square metres and its public toilet awaited him.

25

The suburban railway was deserted early on a Saturday afternoon. Shaken about by the train, Guylain spent the journey time thinking about Julie. What would he do if he actually found her?

'Hello, umm . . . er, my name's Guylain Vignolles, I'm thirty-six years old and I wanted to meet you.' He could not allow himself the luxury of ruining the one chance he might have of making the young woman's acquaintance by stuttering idiotically. There was an alternative solution which was to write a few ardent words in her visitors' book. That might work but it was also taking the risk of seeing his declaration sandwiched between 'Your loos are shit hot!' and 'Toilets nice and clean but the flush is a bit stiff'. The train pulled into the station, jolting Guylain out of his reverie.

Guylain turned up his collar as he came out of the station. There was a chill in the air despite the big, bright sun shining in the sky. The openwork cylindrical metal tower enclosing a big moving red ball with the shopping centre's name on it towered above the rooftops, beckoning him, like a light-house sitting on the town. Évry 2 was less than five minutes' walk away. As soon as he was through the sliding doors, Guylain slowed down, abandoning the brisk pace that had brought him to this point. He felt the urge to spin out this moment and delay the confrontation with the reality against which all his hopes risked being dashed once again.

He strolled idly up the central mall, oblivious of the crowds milling around him. He pictured Julie walking down this same mall first thing in the morning, alone, her footsteps echoing through the vast, empty cathedral. He was at that point in his musings when, above the faint buzz of the horde and the background music blaring out of the loud-speakers suspended from the ceiling, he made out the sound of a waterfall. Close by, a majestic fountain was spewing out its water in continuous heavy jets through the mouths of a group of four marble silurids at its centre. The voice of reason immediately tempered his mounting elation, reminding him that in any self-respecting shopping centre there was a fountain, as there was a children's merry-go-round, a waffle-seller and a central escalator. But he cocked a snook at Miss Killjoy and allowed his heart to skip a beat. The fountain was at the intersection of three main malls, just as Julie had described. Right or left? A woman with a little girl trotted off to the right, the mother entreating the child to hold on, they were almost there. Guylain followed them. As he passed the fountain, he flung into the water of dubious limpidity a nice fat two-euro coin, to ward off bad luck. Less than thirty metres further on, the characteristic toilets sign glowed brightly. Miss Killjoy once again burst into his mind to try and dampen his excitement. Yes, he knew. It just indicated where the toilets were and didn't spell out 'Welcome to Julie, the lavatory attendant's place'. All the same, so far, everything had been exactly as described. A staircase with around fifteen steps led down to the lower ground floor. The place was rang out harshly against the tiled walls. *Peeing is no laughing matter* – Auntologism number 5, Julie's favourite. A second voice, much softer, echoed the words. Even with the interference of all the sounds of flushing, taps and hand-driers, Guylain said to himself that it was the most beautiful voice he had ever heard.

'Peeing is no laughing matter. Sorry I took so long, Aunty, but you know what it's like when Josy cuts my hair. Half an hour for the trim, an hour for a natter.'

Guylain extricated himself from the cubicle and dragged himself over to the washbasins. Turn on the tap, squirt of soap, rub the palms together, lather. His body felt as if it no longer belonged to him. The mirror reflected the face of someone who looked as if they'd seen a ghost. He didn't dare look round at the form on his right, on the periphery of his field of vision. After filling the sink with a mountain of lather, he gave his hands a brief shake, took a deep breath and headed for the exit. Julie was sitting on her chair again and, her head tilted slightly forward, was covering the page of her notebook in her rounded handwriting. Of her face, Guylain only managed to glimpse the regular bridge of her nose, the soft, rounded form of her cheekbones and the slightly fleshy bulge of her lips. The curtain of eyelashes revealed nothing of her eyes. With her free hand, a hand with short, but delicate fingers, she stroked the back of her bare neck. Her hair was the colour of honey, one of those mountain honeys with dark, shimmering glints. She looked up for a second, her gaze focused on the wall opposite, and sucked the tip of her pen before resuming her writing. The sarcastic 'Thank you anyway' that she shouted after him as he left pierced his heart. The only change he'd had on him on arrival at the shopping centre had been lying for nearly ten minutes in the fountain's circular basin beneath fifty centimetres of water. In his head, there was no room for anything other than this revelation: Julie wasn't beautiful, she was sublime.

Outside, the loudspeakers announced between jingles that spring was around the corner. Tuesday 20 March, this coming Tuesday. Guylain smiled. He knew at once what he had to do.

26

When the delivery man turned up, I thought at first that it was a mistake. That the guy had come in the wrong door or that he was just popping into my toilets to relieve an urgent need that wouldn't wait till later. But when he plonked himself in front of me and asked me, chomping away on his chewing gum, if I was Julie, I had no alternative but to stammer a guarded yes. Two seconds later, I found myself holding this crazy thing. I couldn't believe my eyes. A bouquet, here, for me. And what a bouquet! A cascade of fresh flowers that filled almost the entire surface of the table, one of those enormous arrangements with the stems immersed in a big transparent sachet of water. I immediately called Josy, who ditched her customer in the middle of colouring her hair to whizz down and admire the thing. When she saw it, she exclaimed that any guy capable of sending flowers like that could only be either a nutter or the most extraordinary guy on earth. 'Looks like you've hit the jackpot,' she said, her eyes full of envy, before going back to finish her customer's colour and making me promise to tell her everything. This had never happened to me before, such an incredible gesture in such an inappropriate place, nor had it ever happened to my aunt either, in her career spanning nearly forty years. Except the time when, she told me after the event, a gentleman had given her a rose one Valentine's Day, because his girlfriend had just dumped him and he didn't know what to do with the thorny stem that was a nuisance. Stapled to the cellophane around the flowers was this fat brown envelope with the words 'For Julie' written in black ink. My hands were trembling a little when I opened it. The earthenware tile it contained was strangely like my tiles. Same size, same slightly milky colour. Utterly baffled, I turned the tile over and over until I read the handwritten letter that went with it:

JEAN-PAUL DIDIERLAURENT

Dear Ms Julie,

I am not exactly what one might call a Prince Charming. For what it's worth, I find that Prince Charmings all tend to be rather smug, which annoys me and does not particularly endear them to me. I am no Prince Charming, and I have no white steed either. I too sometimes throw coins into fountains when the opportunity arises. I don't have an unsightly wart on my chin, nor do I lisp, but I do have a really stupid name which alone is equal to all the warts and lisps of the world. I love books, even though I spend most of my waking hours destroying them. My worldly goods amount to a goldfish called Rouget de Lisle, and my only friends are a legless cripple who spends his time searching for his limbs, and a versifier who only speaks in alexandrines. I should add that a little while ago, I discovered that in this world there was a person who had the power of making colours brighter, things less serious, winter less harsh, the unbearable more bearable, the beautiful more beautiful, the ugly less ugly . . . in other words, the power to make my life more beautiful. That person, Julie, is you. So even though I'm no fan of speed dating, I am asking you – no, imploring you – to please grant me eight minutes of your life (I find that seven isn't a very attractive number, especially for a date).

So now I must plead guilty. Guilty of having entered your life via this memory stick which I found on the train three weeks ago. But know that if I entered your life in this way, initially it was with the sole intention of finding you so I could return the stick and the writings it contained, even though that intention gradually turned into a profound desire to meet you. So to earn your forgiveness, allow me to give you this additional tile to add to your inventory tomorrow. For, whatever you may think, nothing in life is ever written in stone. Even a number as ugly as 14,717 can one day be transformed into a beautiful number with a little bit of help. I shall end with this expression which, I admit, is a bit pompous but I fear I'll never have the opportunity or the desire to say it to anyone else but you: My fate is in your hands.

It was signed Guylain Vignolles, and underneath was a simple phone number. Maybe this guy was crazy, but he had made me feel very churned up. I shook the envelope and the memory stick fell onto the table. The dark red one. I'd been hunting everywhere for it for *three weeks, since the day I took the train to go to Josy's place. I reread the letter once, then twice. I think I spent the entire day rereading that wretched letter. Returning to it constantly, dipping into it at the slightest opportunity, between wiping down the surfaces and squirts of bleach. Savouring every word, trying to put a face, a voice, to this guy and his stupid name, as he calls it. Today, curiously, the tinkle of the coins in my china saucer sounded different, the hours sped by, the neon light was warmer, and even the people seemed nicer than usual. In the evening, snuggled under my duvet, I read it again from beginning to end, until I knew every word by heart. Before I fell asleep, I knew that I was going to call Guylain Vignolles. I believe I had actually made up my mind before I'd finished reading the letter for the second time. Call him to tell him that it wasn't eight pathetic minutes that I would grant him, but three hours, the time it took me to get to sleep. Three hours to tell me about himself, to tell each other about ourselves, and venture perhaps where our words have never been.*

This morning, the spring equinox, I hummed as I counted my tiles. Guylain Vignolles's tile, tucked in the

With thanks to Ruth Diver
for translating the alexandrines.